SHAME

ON

YOU

FOOL ME ONCE #1

Also by Tara Sivec

Tara Sivec

SHAME ON YOU

FOOL ME ONCE #1

Montlake Romance

The characters and events portrayed in this book are fictitious. Any similarity to real persons, living or dead, is coincidental and not intended by the author.

Text copyright ©2014 by Tara Sivec

Published by Montlake Romance, Seattle

www.apub.com

ISBN-13: 9781477817483
ISBN-10: 1477817484

Cover by Erin Fitzsimmons

Library of Congress Control Number: 2013916304

Printed in the United States of America

To Jasinda, Sterling, and Tiffany, three kick-ass girls who would handcuff me to my steering wheel before they'd let me be a fool.

CHAPTER 1

F ool me once, shame on you. Fool me twice . . . come on, why aren't you guys saying this with me?" Paige McCarty complains. She cocks her gorgeous blonde head to the side and stares us down with her big, crystal-blue eyes.

"Because this is dumb. We do not need to chant our motto every time we get together." I signal the waitress for another round of drinks.

I need booze. Lots and lots of booze to get through this meeting. I love my best friends, but sometimes, I want to punch them in the face. Lovingly, of course.

"Yes, we do, Kennedy O'Brien. We started this company because men are scum-sucking pigs who deserve what's coming to them," Paige says with an angry huff as her bright-pink fruity drink is set down in front of her.

"Thank you so much, you're a doll!" she exclaims to the waitress.

Not only is Paige insanely beautiful, she can flip her moods faster than anyone I've ever seen. At thirty years old, her face has graced the cover of every beauty magazine in existence and she's got the charm of a Southern belle, but don't cross her or she will cut you. And this, folks, is why we are friends.

"I, for one, need to be reminded of why I abhor all things male," Paige tells us as she blots her lip gloss with a cocktail napkin. "All of the money I made modeling was blown on Andy's secret

1

gambling trips. This motto reminds me of how I felt the day I walked into Jimmy Choo and all of my credit cards were declined, and the sense of satisfaction I felt when I went home and set fire to all of Andy's clothes on the front lawn."

A dreamy sigh escapes her heart-shaped mouth when she thinks back on the inferno of revenge, and it reminds me to never get between a model and her need for shoes. Ever. Underneath all that beauty is a brain that is fast thinking, conniving, and perfect for our business.

"I'm certain we will never forget that men are lying, cheating imbeciles." Lorelei Warner brushes off an imaginary piece of lint on her black suit pants. "Gary sent me his wedding invitation yesterday. 'We hope you can join us for the joyous celebration of Gary and Doug as they pledge their endless love to each other.' Can you believe that rat bastard actually invited me?"

Lorelei, my other best friend, means business when she swears. Sure, "rat bastard" isn't up there on the swearing chart, but it is for her. She's actually the type of person who will say, "Cheese and rice!" instead of Jesus Christ.

"See? Lorelei is swearing. The world is coming to an end," Paige laments to me. "If we don't stick together with this motto, she might forget about coming home to find Doug sampling some sweet Italian sausage."

Lorelei makes a gagging noise and covers her mouth with her hand. Unfortunately, Paige isn't talking about food. She's talking about Nuncio, the hot waiter at Villa Macri Ristorante—the place where Doug proposed to Lorelei and where they celebrated their anniversary every year.

Lorelei met Doug at Harvard Law and once they both graduated and were well established in their respective law firms, they tied the knot. I always suspected Doug played for the other team.

He was too pretty. And do you know any straight men who have hair pomade shipped in from Paris?

"What cases do we have on the schedule this week?" I ask as Lorelei pulls out a few files from her leather briefcase now that she's composed herself after remembering the night her ex-husband became a gay man.

"We've got a bail jumper, a cheating spouse, and a subpoena delivery. Who wants what?" Lorelei asks as she sets the files down in the middle of the table so we can flip through them.

"I do believe I've had enough of cheating spouses, so count me out for that one." I grab the bail-jumper file and flip through it. I was trained by Uncle Sam in the army, so firing a gun at bad guys and being in the midst of danger is what I thrive on.

"Speaking of cheating rat bastards, have you talked to Alex lately?" Paige asks as she tests her froufrou drink and finds it to her liking.

"Ha! Yeah, right!" I reply with a snort. Finishing off my Bud Light Lime, I slam the empty glass back onto the table with a clunk. "He was supposed to pick up the girls last weekend and never showed or called. I hope his penis falls off. I hope it rots and falls off inside of Miss Teen USA, therefore causing her perfect, twenty-two-year-old vagina to rot and fall out of her thong when she sneezes."

Paige and Lorelei stare at me with open mouths once I finish with my tirade.

"Wow, tell us how you really feel," Lorelei replies sympathetically with a pat to my arm.

"It's okay. It's fine. I'm perfectly FINE with the fact that while I was fighting for our country, he was fighting to singlehandedly ruin our marriage. What's NOT fine is the fact that he's ignoring his daughters. How did I not know he was a worthless human being when I met him?" I ask with a disgusted shake of my head.

"How did I not know Andy was playing ten-thousand-dollar hands of Texas Hold'em instead of going to software conferences? How did Lorelei not know that Doug likes to play slap and tickle with balls instead of boobs? Because men are rat bastards, that's how," Paige explains.

"Rat bastards," Lorelei and I agree with a nod of our heads.

Continuing my quick scan of the case file, it looks like this should be a pretty easy one to handle. The guy tried to rob a house while the owners were still home. He panicked when he saw them sitting in the kitchen, dropped the laptop he had in his arms, picked up their Chihuahua instead, and bolted out the front door.

He got out on bail and then skipped his court date. Which is a no-no when you use a bail bondsman to help you get out of jail. You should never piss off a bail bondsman. It will always end badly.

In this case, Martin McFadden pissed off my father, who owns Buddy's Bail Bonds, his pride and joy after he retired from the army. All the men in my family served in the army. My grandfather, my Uncle Wally, my two cousins Beaver and Ward (my Aunt Janet loved the TV show *Leave It to Beaver*—don't ask), and both of my older brothers, Bobby and Ted. (Bobby, Ted, Kennedy. Go ahead and get it out of your system now. My Irish-American mother always wanted to be Jackie O, sue me.) My mother died when I was a baby and since I was the only girl, army was all I knew. I enlisted right out of high school just like everyone in my family. Unfortunately, I didn't really do it to make my family happy; I did it to make a boy happy. THE boy. Alex Bradford, my high school sweetheart. I met him in twelfth grade when his father retired from the army and they moved to our small town. We were in gym class together and when I was assigned to his dodgeball team, he leaned down and whispered, "Don't worry, I won't let anyone hit you with any of the balls." It melted my heart and pissed me off all at the same time.

According to the file, the Chihuahua Martin snatched is a two-year-old named Tinkerdoodle that I could punt like a football. He took her from her comfy, pink, bedazzled dog bed, and the owners haven't stopped crying since then. No, he didn't go back for the TV, the jewelry, or the artwork; he went back for a yappy, ankle-biting dog. What an idiot. This will be an easy paycheck for the week, I can feel it.

CHAPTER 2

$\sim\!\!\mathcal{S}\!\!\sim$

Sliding into the front seat of my silver Ford Explorer, I get the SUV started just as my cell phone rings. My dad starts complaining before I even say hello.

"Your uncle is pissing me off this morning. Pick me up a black-cherry slushie on your way in."

While most people need coffee to function properly each day, Buddy O'Brien needs black-cherry slushies from Circle K, the best convenience store in the entire world. I know for a fact that he picks one up every morning on his way to work, so if he's calling me for a second one, it must be bad.

"What did he do now?" I ask with a sigh as I back out of my driveway and head toward Granger, a suburb of South Bend, Indiana, where both of our offices are located.

"He messed up all of my fucking files. I don't know where a GD thing is in this place. Fucking hell."

Word to the wise, my father is a tough guy, but he is Irish Catholic. He will find a way to add the word *fuck* into every single sentence, but he will never, ever take the Lord's name in vain. Hell hath no fury like my father if he hears you say *Goddamn*. When it rains, I can still feel the sting of his hand when he smacked me upside the back of my head the one time I said it when I was twelve and *Scooby-Doo* didn't end the way I wanted it to.

GD Scooby-Doo.

"Why don't you just tell him to stop touching your files," I suggest as I turn onto Heritage Square Drive and make my way to Circle K.

"Is that Kennedy? Tell her you're being unreasonable and that I can't work under these conditions!"

I roll my eyes at Uncle Wally's shout in the background and the fact that my father completely forgets that he's on with me and yells back.

"Do you want to take this outside, Wallace? I will kick your ass into next week!"

"Don't you use that tone with me, you old bastard. You couldn't kick the south side of a barn!"

Finding a parking spot right in front of the store, I set the phone down in the front passenger seat without hanging up. I grab my father's super-size black-cherry slushie and a hazelnut coffee with hazelnut cream for myself. Normally, I drink my coffee black. When you're in the army, you have to get used to the bare essentials. But something tells me I'm going to need a hell of a lot more than just the basics to get through this morning.

Climbing back into my car, I can still hear my father and uncle shouting through the phone line. My father is two years older than Uncle Wally and I have never seen two people fight more, aside from my brothers. Whatever made them think they should work together is beyond me. When my father retired from the army, he opened Buddy's Bail Bonds. Two years later, when Uncle Wally retired, he cashed in his pension, invested the money into the business, and became my father's partner. Once a week, they argue about changing the name to Buddy Wally's Bail Bonds. You would think that since they share the same last name, one of them might be bright enough to make *that* suggestion. O'Brien's Bail Bonds has a nice ring to it. But that would mean the two of them would have to come to a compromise and that's not happening anytime this century.

I find a spot on the street in front of Buddy's and thank the traffic gods that I didn't have to drive around for twenty minutes looking for a place to park. With my coffee and my dad's slushie in my hands, I take a fortifying breath before opening the glass door to the office. I immediately have to duck as a stapler comes flying through the air and crashes into the wall.

"I'm not the dumbass who doesn't know how to alphabetize!"

"Call me a dumbass one more time. Go ahead, do it!"

"DUMBASS!"

Setting the cups on the nearest desk, I rush in between my father and Uncle Wally as they charge toward each other in the middle of the room.

"All right, that's enough! Back to your corners!" I shout at them, pointing in the general direction of their desks, which are on opposite sides of the room.

"He started it," Uncle Wally complains under his breath as he turns and stomps back to his desk.

I swear to God it's like having two more children dealing with these two. A few years ago for Christmas I bought them each a set of boxing gloves. When it gets really bad, I make them go out back and duke it out. This is actually one of the milder arguments and I think we can skip fight club today.

"I need the rest of the information you have on Martin McFadden," I tell my dad as I hand him his slushie and he begins gulping it down while he sifts through a pile of files on top of his desk.

"If your father would have started using my new filing system, he could have e-mailed you that information in three seconds," Uncle Wally muses from his desk.

Dad slams down his cup and starts clenching his fists.

"Can it, Uncle Wally. Dad, just drink your slushie."

With a heavy sigh, he starts slurping through the straw, just to annoy my uncle.

My dad has a few part-time bounty hunters on his payroll and in the past when he got slammed with requests, before I opened Fool Me Once Investigations and I wasn't busy with army duty, he'd have me fill in for him. I love the thrill of the chase and the rush of adrenaline when you find your man (or woman) and slap the cuffs on him (or her). After my marriage went down the shitter six months ago, I decided not to reenlist with the army so I could spend more time with my girls and they wouldn't feel like both parents abandoned them.

"Ahhhh, here we go," my dad states brightly as he finally finds the McFadden file and hands it over to me. "His last known address is in there as well as a list of all of his relatives. I haven't had time to dig any deeper into his criminal background, but I figure Lorelei can pull some strings for you and get whatever else you need. Speaking of Lorelei, how are she and Paige? And when are you going to stop being so stubborn and just come work for me full time instead of just taking a case for me every once in a while?"

I sigh and shake my head at him. "Lorelei and Paige are fine. And we've gone over this a thousand times, Dad. I appreciate the offer of a full-time job, but I need to do something on my own. I need to keep busy so I don't continue filling up notebooks with all of the ways I can remove Alex's penis from his body. While fun, it's not very constructive. Or healthy. Fool Me Once is the perfect distraction for me."

Grabbing the file from my dad's hand, I lean over his desk to kiss his cheek.

"I get it. You need to be independent. Just know, you'll always have a job here if you decide adding things to the penis-removal list is more worthwhile," he says with a smile.

I should have known Dad would be on board with *that* idea. He's the reason I even started the notebooks in the first place. He'd told me the next time he saw Alex he was going to rip his dick off with his bare hands and then smack Alex across the face with the stump.

"Thanks, Dad. We still on for the Notre Dame game this weekend?" I ask as I grab my coffee and start walking backward to the door.

"You bet your sweet ass we are! Kickoff is at noon, so don't be late," my dad warns.

When you live in South Bend, Indiana, and a stone's throw away from the University of Notre Dame, football is a way of life. Every Saturday in the fall is dedicated to watching our favorite team and pigging out on beer and junk food.

"Oh, and I hired a new guy for a few of our cases. He's an excop, so I'm giving him a shot at some bounty-hunter work. He's going to meet you at McFadden's house in thirty minutes so you can show him the ropes. Be nice to him," Dad tells me with a raise of his eyebrow.

I work alone. I've always worked alone. The fact that I own a business with two other women hasn't changed that. We each bring something different to the table and we each have our own separate jobs to do. Alone.

My father knows this and I'm sure he didn't need another bounty hunter, but he hired one anyway to make sure I wouldn't get into any trouble. For some reason, trouble always seems to find me no matter how hard I try to stay away from it.

"Dad, I don't need any help on this case. I'm thirty-five years old and I've fought in Afghanistan, for fuck's sake," I complain as I shake my head at him.

"Humor me, Kennedy. I'm old. I'm going to die soon. I'd like to die knowing you'll be safe."

My dad has many skills. But his best one is his guilt trips. He is as healthy as a horse and the most stubborn human being on the face of the earth. He isn't going to die anytime soon. He'll outlive cockroaches and Twinkies.

I throw my hand in the air in an irritated wave and head back outside to my car. I swear to God if this guy doesn't stay out of my way or screws anything up on this job, I will take my dad out back and beat his ass myself.

GD newbie bounty hunters.

CHAPTER 3

⌒

I pull up to the address for Martin McFadden and even though I googled the area and I'm a little familiar with the neighborhood, I'm still a bit surprised that this is the house of the criminal I'm hunting. It's not the typical residence of a person I'm tracking down. Those people lean more toward houses on wheels with Spider-Man bedsheets for curtains and one-room apartments that make crack houses look like the lap of luxury.

This house looks like a sweet, little old lady lives here, not a bail-jumping criminal. It's a ranch with a gorgeous white wrap-around porch and there are hanging baskets of flowers all along the railing. As I get out of my vehicle, I notice the lawn has been manicured right down to those crisscross patterns you see on baseball fields. I make my way up the front walk and when I see a decorative flag stuck in the ground by the porch steps that says "Welcome Friends!" I'm once again bolstered by the fact that bringing this guy in will be a piece of cake.

According to the file, he's fifty years old, has never been married, and is kind of a hermit. I get to the top step and the loud rumble of a motorcycle has me whipping my head around and my hand automatically going for my gun. I didn't see anything in the notes about McFadden owning a motorcycle, but you can never be too sure about these things.

I watch as a Heritage Softail Classic Harley pulls to a stop right in front of the house and feel my insides quiver. Even though this guy is wearing a helmet and I haven't seen his face yet, I can already tell this isn't my guy. McFadden is five foot five and a hundred twenty-five pounds soaking wet; this guy is wearing a tight, white T-shirt and the muscles in his biceps tighten as he clutches the handlebars and swings his leg over the seat of the bike.

With his back to me while he pockets the bike key, I have time to appreciate him. And by appreciate, I mean ogle. I'm staring at his ass and I'm not ashamed to admit it. Whoever this guy is, he has an amazing ass. I watch as he reaches up and slides his helmet off and I take note of the way his shirt stretches across the muscles of his back.

I need to get laid. I really, really need to get laid. I'm standing on the front porch of a bail jumper's house panting like a dog.

This must be the guy my father hired. I can see his service pistol secured in the waistband of his jeans at his back. It's a Beretta M9—the exact same gun I use. Maybe my father had the right idea hiring this guy. I don't need the help, but at least he'll be pretty to look at. And maybe if he's lucky, I'll throw him a bone. Or he can throw me *his* bone. My girly bits tingle just thinking about being anywhere near this guy and his bone.

"Come on, pretty boy. Turn around so I can see your face," I whisper to myself as he secures his helmet to the back of the bike and finally turns to face me.

All thoughts of bones, humping, and great asses fly out the window and my mouth drops open in complete and utter shock.

This isn't happening. This is SO not happening right now.

The corner of his mouth tips up in a panty-dropping grin, showcasing the dimple on his left cheek, and I want to stomp my feet and throw a temper tantrum right now because he *knows* I was staring at his ass. He knows I was standing here on this porch thinking about all of the dirty things I could do to him. He knows it and he's enjoying every minute of it, the rat bastard.

"What the hell are you doing here?" I shout angrily as I stomp down the steps and meet him in the middle of the sidewalk.

"It's nice to see you too, gorgeous. It's been a while."

Griffin Crawford. My ex-husband's best friend and the guy I once had a massive crush on in high school. Even though I never did anything stupid like act on my attraction to him back in the day, he still knew. Somehow, he knew and he used it to piss me off on a regular basis. Griffin went to high school with me and Alex and he also followed us into the army. On my last tour in Afghanistan, it was Griffin whom I spent months with in the desert, fighting for our lives. It was Griffin whom I confided in that I thought something was off with Alex back home. It was Griffin who convinced me that Alex and I were just going through a rough patch, and that once I got back home, everything would be fine, and we'd work things out.

A few months after I kicked Alex's sorry, cheating ass out of the house, I found out Griffin knew about the affair the entire time.

He knew and he had let me cry on his shoulder wondering what the hell was wrong. He let me pour my heart out to him day after day and he never said a word. Childish teasing aside, through the years, Griffin became one of *my* best friends too. You would think that would guarantee me a little bit of loyalty. But obviously, since I don't have a penis, I wasn't cool enough for the truth.

"Don't call me gorgeous and don't waltz in here like it's no big deal," I growl at him. "I don't know what angle you're playing at by getting my father to hire you, but you can just get your ass back on that bike. I am NOT working with you."

Griffin takes a step closer to me and pushes his hands into the front pockets of his jeans.

"Are you referring to the ass you were staring at when I pulled up? I just want to make sure I'm understanding you correctly," he says with that stupid, cocky grin.

"Oh, get over yourself! I have a job to do and I don't need you fucking everything up. I prefer to work with honest, loyal people. Not backstabbing, lying assholes," I fire at him.

I'm actually shocked to see the cockiness wiped right off his face, replaced by a look of regret and anger as he stares down at me.

"I never lied to you, Kennedy. I was in the dark about Alex just as much as you were. If you stopped avoiding me and ignoring all my calls and texts at any point over the last few months, I could have explained it to you," he tells me, moving even closer until I have to crane my neck to see his face.

I'm pretty tall, but Griffin towers over me at six foot four. Alex and I are the exact same height. Maybe that's why I always felt more safe and protected when I was in combat with Griffin. Or when I was anywhere in the same vicinity as him. Griffin always has a five-o'clock shadow and I've never seen him in anything other than a T-shirt, jeans, and shit-kicker boots. Where pretty boy Alex is a lover (of anything with a vagina), Griffin is a fighter and intimidates everyone he comes in contact with. Except for me.

If he didn't have such a big attitude and so many muscles, I'd say he could pass for a surfer boy with his blue eyes and dark blond hair that he usually keeps military short, but it had grown out a bit on top since the last time I'd seen him.

"You tried to feed me that same bullshit six months ago, remember? I didn't believe it then and I sure as hell don't believe it now. Are you forgetting about the fact that I *heard* you? I heard you talking to him. I listened to you tell him not to say anything to me."

I can feel myself starting to get choked up as I remember the day I walked into Griffin's house a few hours after I'd seen Alex with the nanny. Alex had no idea I'd seen him. I was too stunned to do anything other than run back out of the house and drive around aimlessly. When I came back to my senses, I immediately went to Griffin's house to get his advice. I walked into Griffin's kitchen that day and overheard him talking to Alex on the phone. I stood there while Griffin advised my husband to continue to lie to me about the affair and never, ever tell me the truth. I thought my heart was broken when I found out Alex had been screwing around on me, but it was nothing compared to having one of your best friends deceive you.

"Kennedy, that's not how—"

I cut him off and cross my arms angrily in front of me. "Oh, shut the hell up! I don't want to listen to your excuses."

"And you don't want to listen to reason either. You shut me out for six months, but enough is enough. We are going to hash this out once and for all. I'm not going anywhere this time, Kennedy."

Turning my back on him so I don't have to see his face, I walk away and head back toward the front porch so I can case the house and see if McFadden has been back here since he skipped out on his court date.

"Go away, Griffin. I don't need your help on this job and I sure as hell don't need you in my life," I shout over my shoulder.

No sooner have the words left my mouth than gunshots ring out from somewhere in the house. I don't even have time to reach for my gun before I'm tackled from behind and pushed down into the grass. Griffin's body completely covers mine and his arms shield my head as shots echo above us for a few more seconds. When silence finally descends on the neighborhood, I feel Griffin slowly push himself up off me just enough so I can roll over underneath him.

This was a bad decision. A really bad decision considering how pissed I am at him and how sex deprived I am right now. Our bodies are touching from feet to chest and I can feel every inch of his hard, muscled body on top of mine. It's been a long time since I've had a man's body pressing into me and I am not happy with how good it feels right now.

Griffin is hot. I've always thought he was hot, but he was my friend. Friend only, because even though I may have had a silly crush on him at one point, I was already dating Alex and obviously I had better morals than Alex did. And now, Griffin is no longer my friend because he lied to me.

Someone needs to get that message to my vagina because she isn't having any of this "I'm pissed off at Griffin and want nothing to do with him" nonsense. Her engine is running and she's screaming at me to shift into high gear.

I swallow thickly and look up into Griffin's face. He's scanning the yard and the house to find the threat and I can't help but stare at his throat and chiseled jaw and wonder what his skin tastes like.

Jesus, what the hell is wrong with me? Am I that desperate that I would lie here in the grass after being shot at and fantasize about my ex–best friend? Thirty seconds with this man and I've already lost my freaking mind.

The sounds of a crash and squealing tires pull my attention away from the man above me and I crane my neck to see a red Honda Civic crashing through the closed garage door of McFadden's house. The man behind the wheel, whom I assume is McFadden because of the tiny little Chihuahua sitting on his lap, screams at us as he floors it backward out of the driveway and into the street.

"YOU'LL NEVER TAKE ME ALIVE!"

His threat is punctuated by a short, yippy bark from Tinkerdoodle before he throws the car out of reverse and takes off down the residential street.

"So, what was that you were saying about not needing help on this job?" Griffin asks, the cocky grin back on his face as he stares down at me and makes no move to get the hell off me.

Placing my palms flat on his muscled chest, I shove him roughly away until he rolls to the side. I scramble up from the ground, wiping grass and dirt off my jeans and out of my hair before stalking across the yard toward my car.

"So, I guess I'll talk to you later and we can go over our strategy?" he yells with a chuckle as I get in my car and angrily slam the door closed without answering him.

I am never going to be able to get any work done with him around, trying to worm his way back into my life.

GD Griffin Crawford.

CHAPTER 4

❦

I walk through the door of Fool Me Once Investigations and avoid my friends' stares at the condition I've returned to the office in as I sit down at my desk. I realize my hair is filled with grass and my clothes are dirty and askew, but I was kind of hoping they wouldn't notice.

"Boy, I could use some more coffee. Did anyone make a pot?" I ask as I drum my fingers on top of my desk, waiting for my Mac to come to life.

Neither of them answer me and I can see them looking at me out of the corner of my eye. Just act natural. Nothing to see here, folks.

"I'm in the mood to go shopping. Maybe buy some new shoes!" I exclaim.

Shit! I hate shopping. What the hell am I saying?

"Ha ha, just kidding! Shopping is dumb. We should sign up for a cooking class. Wouldn't that be great?!"

What? NO! STOP TALKING!

"So no one made any coffee? I think I'll make a pot. Who wants a cup?" I ask in a rush as I get up from my desk and make a beeline for the kitchenette in the back of the office.

Paige intercepts me halfway, her eyes narrowing as she looks me over from head to toe.

"Oh my God! Why do you have leaves in your hair? Sweet Jesus. Lorelei, get Sven on the phone, I can see Kennedy's roots."

Son of a bitch.

I don't have time to sit in a chair for four hours and listen to Sven tell me about his Yorkshire terrier, Mrs. Justin Bieber, and her bowel movements. That dog is as dumb as her namesake. She walks in circles until she gets so dizzy that she falls down. Like those fainting goats on YouTube. Her legs go all stiff and then she just falls to her side and Sven leaves me in my chair with enough foils on my head to communicate with Mars to go running up to her in a screaming panic telling people to call 911. Then the dumbass dog immediately jumps up and starts the process all over again. Mrs. Justin Bieber is an asshole.

"Sorry, I have to be in court in twenty minutes," Lorelei states, getting up from her own desk and walking toward me. "What happened?"

I do my own shrugging in response and continue with the act that this is just a regular day at the office. A regular day of being shot at and snuggling in the grass with a guy who makes my blood boil.

"Hey, I need you to pull up whatever information you can find on McFadden. My dad didn't have time to get everything." Time to change the subject.

"I figured as much. Here you go," she tells me, handing me a file filled with papers. "Now, back to the issue at hand. Or should I say, tree bark in hair. What happened?"

Taking the file from her hand, I make a production of flipping through the pages, oohing and ahhing at what I see as she stands there tapping her high-heeled foot on the floor.

"Thanks, Lo. Speaking of the bail jumper, how about we switch cases? I think it's about time you got your feet wet out in the field," I tell her as Paige begins pulling leaves and grass out of my hair, mumbling to herself about wasted beauty.

Lorelei snorts, shaking her head. "Nice try. I'm pretty sure we have a rule somewhere in our mission statement about how each individual assigned to a case will see the entire thing through, right, Paige?"

Paige nods her head absently as she gives me a reassuring pat on the back before noticing another grass stain by my hip.

"Thou shalt not covet thy friend's cases. Why do you want to trade?"

I smack Paige's hands away from my hip and shoot her a dirty look.

"Really? The Ten Commandments are in our mission statement?" I ask irritably.

"Why are you changing the subject?" Lorelei demands.

Because I cannot work with Griffin.

"Because this is going to be a pretty boring, easy case. Perfect for one of you to handle to get some experience behind you," I lie.

"A boring, easy case doesn't usually involve coming back to the office looking like roadkill," Paige says.

"Gee, thank you so much," I tell her sarcastically.

"Fresh roadkill, but roadkill nonetheless," she replies with a shrug. "Spill it."

I can question insurgents in the middle of war-torn Afghanistan, but I am no match for these two. It only takes a few seconds of their stare-down before I cave.

"I WAS SHOT AT! I saw my life flash before me!"

Lorelei rolls her eyes at me. "You love being shot at—it gives you a cheap thrill. Try again."

GD friends.

"FINE! Griffin Crawford showed up at McFadden's house. On a HARLEY. And dove on top of me to protect me when McFadden started shooting. And my father hired him to work on this case. Can you believe that? My own father is a traitor."

Paige lets out a low whistle under her breath. "A Harley? Oh, man. You're screwed."

"She speaks the truth," Lorelei adds as she grabs her leather briefcase and Coach purse and moves toward the door. "You've watched every season of *Sons of Anarchy* thirty-seven times and instead of porn hidden under your mattress, you have *American Iron* and Harley-Davidson's *HOG* magazines. You're definitely screwed."

Lorelei blows us a kiss as she exits the office to get to court and I turn to face Paige with a sigh.

"So, what kind of bike does he have?" she asks.

"Oh my God, it's a Heritage Softail Classic with a Twin Cam engine, laced wheels with whitewalls, and studded leather. It's beautiful," I tell her as I close my eyes and picture the bike in my head. The bike with me on the back of it, my body draped around Griffin, and my arms clutching his waist.

Shit!

"What the hell am I supposed to do? I can't work with Griffin," I complain.

"You're right. You're absolutely right. There is no way you can work with that man under these conditions. It's a tragedy and I am going to do something about it." Paige grabs her cell phone from her desk and starts scrolling through her contacts.

What would I do without my friends? Seriously? I knew Paige wouldn't let me down. I know my father gave me this case and transferring it to another firm is going to piss him off, but he'll just have to deal with it. Paige understands what a bad idea it would be for me to be anywhere near Griffin, Harley or no Harley. I don't trust him. I can't work with someone I don't trust. Especially when he's a cocky smartass with too many muscles. And a Harley. A fucking Harley.

"Hello, darling, it's Paige," she says into her phone. "I need your help. It's an emergency."

I can always count on my friends. This makes me feel warm and fuzzy to know she's got my back.

"No, not for me, for Kennedy," she continues, before turning to face me and staring me up and down before shaking her head sadly at me.

What the hell is she doing? She doesn't need to look at me like that just to call another PI firm a few towns over for some additional help.

"Yes, I think it has to be today. She can't go on like this anymore," Paige adds. "Perfect! You are a lifesaver. Kiss, kiss. We'll see you in twenty."

Paige hangs up the phone and walks around her desk to retrieve her purse from one of the drawers.

"Why do we need to go see the guys at Osborne Investigations? Can't they just send someone over so I can fill them in on the case?"

Paige pulls her keys out of her purse and walks back over to me, linking her arm through mine and pulling me toward the door.

"What are you talking about? I didn't call Osborne. I called Sven. Your roots are atrocious. There's no way I'm letting you anywhere near Griffin Crawford again with hair like that."

She clutches my arm with both hands when she feels me start to resist, I don't even bother hiding my contempt by calling her every bad name I can think of from *A* to *Z*, starting with *asshat* and ending with . . .

GD zoo animal cray-cray.

CHAPTER 5

G et away from me, you little rat," I whisper to Mrs. Justin Bieber as she sniffs the toe of my boot and then walks away in an angry huff.

I glare at Paige as she happily chats up Sven a few feet away, hoping she'll feel my stare of death and get me the hell out of here. I don't have time for this. I have a bail jumper to catch and a Harley man to get rid of.

I reach my fingers up to the neckband of the black plastic cape and tug on it, trying to relieve some of the choking sensation. My head itches like crazy so I use one of my fingernails to dig in between the foils.

"Don't touch anysing. Vhat is vrong viff you. You mess up my masterpiece," Sven scolds as he walks over to me, smacks my hand away, and lifts up some of the foils on my head to check them.

I know for a fact Sven's name is really Steve and he was born and raised in Jersey. Every time he speaks I want to borrow a page out of my dad's handbook, smack him upside the head, and ask him what the hell is wrong with him.

"Can you please remoof da gun? It making me so nervous. You shoot Sven on accident," he tells me with a nervous shiver as he stares down at my gun in its holster at my hip.

"How much longer is this going to take? I have work to do," I complain as I unclip my gun and holster and set it on the tray of unused foils next to me.

"Beauty takes time, Kennedy. Be a good girl and maybe I'll take you out for ice cream when we're finished," Paige says with a smile.

Is it illegal for me to pull my gun in the middle of a salon? I need to check the rules of my CCW permit.

"Here, why don't you read through McFadden's file while you're sitting there so patient and well behaved." Paige picks up the folder on the floor by my feet and drops it into my lap.

While Sven walks over to the front desk and Paige flips through a magazine next to me, I watch as Mrs. Justin Bieber whizzes on the floor in the middle of the room. Rolling my eyes, I suck it up and try to get some work done while I'm slowly tortured to death with foil and hair color.

Flipping through the pages of the life and times of Martin McFadden, I almost can't believe what I'm seeing. This guy *is* nuts. According to what Lorelei found in his court records, he's been to jail twenty-two times for making erroneous phone calls to the police. Phone calls about tiny little green men from Mars that were trying to break into his house and eat his brain. Two years ago he was arrested outside of a costume shop at Halloween, screaming at anyone who would listen that if they bought alien costumes, it would anger the little men and they would kill us all. Six months ago he petitioned for a patent for his "Alien Safety Helmet," a pile of tinfoil that he believes should be mandatory for all citizens to wear to protect them from their thoughts being stolen in the middle of the night. He even wrote a book called *They're Reading Our Minds, Watching Us Sleep.*

Sweet Jesus. This is the guy I have to track down?

As I continue reading, I hear the bell as the door opens and someone asks if they handle dog grooming. As I continue to read and try to ignore the conversation going on by the reception desk, I hear a word that makes me whip my head up and my eyes bug out of my head: *Tinkerdoodle.*

My eyes meet McFadden's across the room as he cradles a trembling brown Chihuahua in his arms. I didn't get a very good look at him when he sped off in his Honda, but I have one of his mug shots and it's definitely my guy. If he hadn't already shot at me, I'd say he looks harmless. Almost like a professor of literature with his dark brown corduroy pants, blue button-down shirt, and light brown, cable-knit sweater, his brown hair graying at the temples.

Even with all the foil on top of my head and the cape draped around me, he recognizes me immediately and lets out an ear-piercing shriek before turning and running for the door.

"SON OF A BITCH!" I shout as I scramble to get out of the chair. My feet immediately get caught in the yards of plastic cape and I land in a cursing heap on the floor.

"PAIGE, STOP HIM!" I shout to my friend as she immediately bursts into action and easily leaps over Mrs. Justin Bieber in her four-inch Manolo Blahniks and runs toward the door. McFadden shoves Sven out of the way and into a shelf of hair products and everything comes crashing to the ground, Sven included.

Even though he's lying in a pile of shampoo and conditioner, Sven reaches out with one arm and grabs McFadden's pant leg to try and keep him in place while Paige makes her way closer by kicking hair products out of her way with her heels.

Pushing myself up off the floor, I race across the room as McFadden continues to go for the door, dragging Sven across the floor on his belly behind him while Mrs. Justin Bieber begins yapping and racing around in circles. I watch Paige easily jumping through the maze of fallen bottles and almost grab him when her heel punctures a shampoo bottle and she stops to try and kick it loose. With Paige distracted, McFadden sees me coming for him and starts grabbing anything he can find and pitching it at us one-handed as he heads for the door. Aerosol tins of hairspray fly past my head and Paige takes a gallon jug of conditioner to the shoulder before Sven finally loses his hold on McFadden's pant leg.

"MAN DOWN! MAN DOWN!" Sven screams hysterically as Paige and I jump over his body and fly out of the door right behind McFadden, poor Tinkerdoodle shaking in fear in his arms as he runs.

When we get out onto the sidewalk, I quickly scan every direction until I spot him sprinting full speed to his Honda parked along the curb a block away. I take off at a dead run, my black cape flying behind me like I'm a superhero and I hear Paige's heels smacking against the cement as she races behind me.

"STOP! MCFADDEN!" I scream as I race down the sidewalk and watch him jump into his vehicle and start it up.

He peels out of his parking spot and does a U-turn in the middle of the street, pulling his car right up to Paige and me as we stand there trying to catch our breath.

"You're wearing my Alien Safety Helmet!" he exclaims through his open window as he stares in awe at the foil on my head. "You believe! I feel like under different circumstances, we could really be friends."

Stepping down off the curb, I reach for my gun in its side holster, but quickly realize Sven made me take the fucking thing off.

"SHIT!" I yell in frustration as my hands get tangled in the plastic. "McFadden, don't you dare move. Get out of the car right now. You skipped bail and stole someone's dog."

Tinkerdoodle lets out a high-pitched yap and McFadden cradles the dog to his chest.

"They didn't appreciate her! She's my best friend. YOU'LL NEVER TAKE HER AWAY FROM ME!" he screams before gunning the car and taking off down the street.

He's too far away at this point for me to take a shot at one of his tires to slow him down even if I did have my gun on me. And as I glance around and see all of the people out on the sidewalk watching what just happened, I assume they wouldn't have appreciated me firing my gun at a car in the middle of the day anyway.

I can hear sirens in the distance. Sven must have called the police. I can't believe that idiot was right there in front of us and we didn't get him. This is appalling. Thankfully, my brother Ted and my cousin Ward both work for the local police department so the odds are pretty good that one of them will show up. And if I threaten their lives, they'll keep this whole thing a secret. No one needs to know that I had my bail jumper within arm's reach and couldn't get him because I was getting my hair highlighted. I would never live that shit down.

"I can't believe that asshole got away," Paige complains with her hands on her hips as she stares off down the street.

Turning toward her, I look down at her shoes in awe. "How in the hell did you run so fast in those things?"

"That was nothing. Try being at a Gucci sample sale. Those bitches will cut you if you're not fast," she says with a shrug.

As we turn to make my way back to the salon, the rumbling sound of a Twin Cam Harley engine makes me freeze in place. I slowly turn around.

GD McFadden.

CHAPTER 6

Y ou really shouldn't have prettied yourself up just for me,"
Griffin says with a laugh as he saunters over to me.

Catching my reflection in the storefront window next to me,
I realize I still have foils in my hair and they are sticking up in every
direction. Not to mention the splendid cape that's draped around
my body making it look like I'm a member of McFadden's Anti-
Martian army.

Wonderful. Just wonderful.

"Why are you here?" I mutter through clenched teeth as I stand
up as straight as I can and pretend like the fact that I'm out on the
sidewalk looking like an ass in front of this man doesn't bother me
in the least.

"I heard the news on my police scanner. Figured I'd stop by
and commend you on catching our criminal. But I'm assuming by
the pissed-off look on your face that he got away," he mocks.

"McFadden is not *our* criminal. He's *my* criminal. I already
told you I don't need your help. He caught me by surprise, that's
all. I wasn't expecting him to show up at a salon in broad daylight."

If he doesn't stop smirking at me, I'm going to rip this stupid
cape off, wrap it around his neck, and choke the life out of him.

"Since when do you go to salons? I thought you wouldn't be
caught dead in one of these places," he questions. I can see him

pressing down hard on his lips, his eyes glancing to my hair and then quickly back to my eyes.

"I don't go to these places. I have friends who go to these places and drag me here against my will. And it's just highlights, nothing drastically life changing. Golden blonde highlights that will bring out the gold specks in my eyes."

Overshare much, Kennedy?

"You don't need highlights for that. Your eyes are gorgeous enough all on their own," he says softly as he looks into said gorgeous eyes.

Holy hell, is it hot out here or is it just me? And what the devil is he playing at, flirting with me like this? Yes, I said *flirting* and I realize how outrageous that sounds. Griffin Crawford is fucking flirting with me. I've known him long enough to know when he's turning on the charm. I've seen him charm the underwear right off a stranger in two point three seconds just by complimenting her legs. My underwear is staying right where it is, thank you very much.

Before I can tell him exactly what I think about him and his stupid gorgeous-eyes compliment, a police cruiser pulls up to the curb next to us. I thank my lucky stars when I see my cousin Ward get out and come around to stand next to us.

"Nice hairstyle, Kennedy. Trying to make a phone call to your motherland?" Ward asks with a laugh as he reaches up and flicks one of the foils on my head.

Never mind. I take back my thankfulness.

"Kiss my ass, Ward. I've had a bad fucking day."

I know what you're saying to yourself right now: this sounds like June Cleaver finally had enough of Beaver and the gang's shit.

Ward can see by the look on my face that he should leave me alone. I won't hesitate to put him in a headlock in the middle of the sidewalk. I don't care if he is wearing his police uniform.

"Griffin, my man! How've you been?" Ward asks, turning his attention away from me.

"Can't complain," Griffin replies as the two men exchange handshakes and start talking back and forth about Notre Dame's upcoming season. As teenagers and into early adulthood, we all hung out together: my brothers, my cousins, Griffin, Alex, and me. We were all close in age and we all had the army in common so it naturally made us friends.

The fact that my brothers and my cousins are still friendly with Griffin when he screwed me over pisses me off. They should hate him on principle. If some woman came into my family's lives and stomped all over their hearts, I would cut that bitch. Where's the damn loyalty?

"Excuse me, I hate to interrupt this bromance, but we have work to do." I glare at my cousin.

"I'm sorry, it is impossible to take you seriously right now with all that shit on your head," Ward says, laughing.

I take a step in his direction, preparing myself for a mind-erasing headlock when Griffin lightly touches my arm.

"Before you kill him, we need to talk," Griffin tells me.

"We have nothing to talk about. I'm going to go inside and get this crap out of my hair and then I'm going to get to work. You can just get your ass back on that bike and go find someone else to annoy," I tell him as I turn and fling the door to the salon open angrily.

As soon as I walk inside I'm met by the sounds of wails and barking. Sven is still sitting on the floor in a pile of hair products while Paige attempts to console him, and Mrs. Justin Bieber is losing her shit, barking at anything in her general vicinity and stopping every ten seconds to piss on the floor.

"I ALMOST DIED, PAIGE! It was HORRIBLE! I have so many regrets. So many things I've never accomplished. I'M TOO YOUNG TO DIE!"

I wonder if anyone else notices that in the midst of Sven's hysterics he seems to have forgotten he has an accent. Paige is crouched down next to Sven and pats him on the back at the appropriate times. She catches my gaze and rolls her eyes in annoyance.

"There, there, Sven. You're okay. Look, Kennedy is back!" she exclaims, getting up from her spot on the floor and rushing over to me, lowering her voice so only I can hear her. "I'm going to punch him in his face if he doesn't stop whining."

Taking a deep breath, I move away from Paige and over to Sven's spot on the floor.

"Sven, you did really good under pressure. You almost had that guy!" I tell him so he'll quit the damn crying.

Sven sniffles and wipes his nose on the sleeve of his shirt.

"I did do vell, didn't I? I always sought I should haff been a cop. I haff all of dees natural eenstincts," he tells me seriously, in full-on Germedishithuanian, or wherever-the-hell-he-thinks-he's-from accent.

It takes everything in me not to laugh in his face, but I have to rein it in. I need this guy to fix my hair, pronto.

"Yes, you're absolutely right. How about you get up off the floor and take these foils out of my hair while my cousin Ward questions you?" I ask as Ward walks through the door.

"Oooooh, a man in uniform! I veel better already," Sven exclaims as he takes in my cousin from head to toe before jumping up off the floor and extending his hand out to him, wrist cocked, like he wants Ward to kiss the top of his hand. "My name eez Sven. I am zee one who almost captured zee criminal."

Paige and I share a look of annoyance before turning back to watch Ward awkwardly grab Sven's hand and shake it like a limp noodle.

While Sven begins to regale my cousin with his act of heroism, the bell chimes above the door and I turn to see Griffin walk in.

"Out! Get out!" I raise my hand and point to the door.

"I'm not going anywhere until you talk to me," Griffin replies firmly.

I don't even acknowledge his words. I turn my back on him and drag Sven back toward the shampoo bowls as Ward follows us and continues to ask Sven questions about whether or not he'd ever seen McFadden in the shop before and if McFadden mentioned anything about where he was staying.

Getting comfortable in the reclining seat with my head in the bowl, I close my eyes and try to relax as Sven begins removing foils while talking to Ward. I'm assuming Griffin finally got the hint, but a few seconds later when Sven is running warm water through my hair and massaging my head, I realize Griffin wouldn't get the hint if it ran him over with a Mack truck.

"You can't avoid me forever," Griffin whispers close to my ear.

Too close. I can feel his breath against my neck and it makes me grit my teeth when I feel goose bumps on my arms. Can't he see I'm trying to relax here? He needs to leave me the hell alone. I may not be able to avoid him forever, like he says, but I sure as hell can refuse to talk to him until he goes away.

"Fine, if you don't want to talk now, we can do it later," he states before standing up to his full height and then turning to leave.

As Sven finishes washing my hair and wraps a towel around my head, I avoid smirking to myself as I see Griffin walk away.

The power of my ignoring skills cannot be beat. We all know that when a man says he'll do something "later," it will never, ever be completed. I actually find myself smiling as I walk over to Sven's station so he can spray and brush and flat-iron and all that other shit that usually makes me cringe. Right now, Sven can do whatever he wants to me. Griffin has gotten the hint and is finally walking away.

I don't realize I'm staring at Griffin's ass as he walks away until I'm not looking at his ass anymore. I'm looking at the general vicinity of Paige's crotch as she steps into my line of vision.

I look up at her with a scowl and she raises her eyebrows at me. "I saw that, so don't try to deny it."

I pretend like I have no idea what she's talking about as Sven fires up the blow dryer and goes to town on my hair.

"Saw what? There's nothing to see here," I argue.

"Oh, nonsense," Sven butts in. "Ve all saw you looking at hees ass."

Paige laughs as I glare at her.

"Don't be angry, Kennedy. It's a very nice ass. What I'd like to know is, why, in all the conversations we've had about your dear, old friend Griffin, have you never mentioned what a fine specimen that man is?" Paige demands, putting her hands on her hips.

"Griffin? Good-looking? Pshaw," I reply, brushing off her comment.

Griffin isn't good-looking. Griffin is hot as balls. But Paige doesn't need to know that I know that she knows I know that. Holy hell, I may have had this hair dye in my hair too long.

"Don't give me that bullshit, Kennedy O'Brien. Your eyes got all dreamy when he was bent over whispering in your ear just a second ago," she fires back.

"My eyes did *not* get all dreamy! I don't do dreamy!" I shout above the noise of the hair dryer.

Mrs. Justin Bieber waddles over at this point, stands by my feet, and then yaps at me. One short, high-pitch *yipe*.

"See? Mrs. Justin Bieber even know you lying," Sven adds.

"Look, I get that he pissed you off. You thought he was your friend and he did something that hurt you. But he's trying. He wants to talk to you and maybe it's time you give him a chance to tell him his side of the story. If you won't, I will. Of course, that man

won't have time to talk if I have a few minutes alone with him."
Paige licks her lips as she stares at the door through which Griffin
exited moments ago.

If my hair wasn't wrapped around a brush right now and I
didn't fear losing a large chunk of it by yanking away, I would
spring from this chair and smack the horny right off her face. Just
the idea of Griffin and Paige alone in a room together doing everything *but* talking makes me want to throw up in my mouth a little.
Just because I'm pissed at the guy doesn't mean I want him anywhere near one of my friends. My hot model friend who has never
had a bad-hair day in her life and never stood in front of a person
after months of not speaking to him with foil in her hair, looking
like an idiot.

Griffin is going to go back to whatever hole he crawled out of,
I'm going to catch McFadden *on my own*, and I am never, ever
going to get caught ogling that man's ass ever again.

GD fine ass.

CHAPTER 7

"But Mooooooom, everyone is going to be at Stephanie's party. Why can't I go?" my oldest daughter, Meadow, whines.

"Because you're *twelve*. Do you know what kind of twelve-year-olds go to co-ed parties when there aren't any parents home? Slutty ones, that's who," I inform her as I put the last of the supper dishes into the dishwasher.

Meadow is going to be the death of me. I thought having two daughters was going to be trying enough considering I know nothing about being girly. Thank God I have Paige and Lorelei now. At least they can take her shopping when she doesn't like the jeans and T-shirts I pick out for her. I know you're not supposed to force your children to be like you, but come on, what parent doesn't at least try?

I put her in karate class when she was four and she spent the entire six-week lesson doing pirouettes around the other kids and breaking out into random dance moves instead of kicking some ass. I gave her all of my old G.I. Joe guys to play with when she was six and she gave them all makeovers with nail polish and glitter glue. G.I. Joe can never show his face in the line of duty again. When she turned seven I finally had to suck it up and buy her *a Barbie*.

"Oh my GOD, you are ruining my life!" Meadow screeches at me before stomping out of the kitchen.

"YOU'RE WELCOME!" I shout in reply.

Seriously, she'll thank me one day when she's paying a shrink and getting her money's worth.

Heading over to the fridge, I grab a much-needed bottle of beer and before I can take my first sip, I'm interrupted by a sigh behind me.

Turning around, I see my youngest daughter, Livia, staring up at me with the same annoyed look on her face that I'm sure I have. Yes, I named my daughters after characters on *The Sopranos*. It's in my blood to name my offspring after famous people.

"Meadow is in her room screaming about how much her life sucks. Can we trade her in for a new sister?"

Livia is nine and so much like me it's scary. Everyone calls her my mini-me. Not only does she look exactly like me with long, wavy auburn hair, but she also hates the color pink, her favorite movie is *Full Metal Jacket,* and on her Christmas list last year, she asked Santa for a Wenger Ueli Steck Special Edition Swiss Army knife.

I'm not gonna lie; I cried a few tears when I saw that at the top of the list.

"No, we cannot trade your sister in for a new model. It's just a phase. She'll get over it."

I hope.

"Why does she want to go to a party with boys anyway? Boys are dumb. And gross," Livia replies.

Amen, sister.

Boys are definitely dumb. Especially Alex. He was supposed to pick up the girls tonight and take them to dinner but cancelled at the last minute. Via text. He couldn't even be decent enough to call and tell me, the rat bastard. Meadow immediately tried to take advantage of the situation by telling me that the only thing that would fix her devastation at being stood up by her father was to go to a party. It was a nice try on her part, but I wasn't born yesterday.

Livia, never one to let something like that ruin her day, just shrugged and asked what was for dinner.

Before I can sit Livia down and explain to her all the reasons that boys suck and why she should stay away from them forever, the doorbell rings. For a second as I leave Livia in the kitchen to go answer the door, I actually think it's Alex, coming over to beg forgiveness from the girls and trying to be a stand-up guy.

I should have known better.

Checking the peephole, I groan when I see Griffin standing on the front porch and fling the door open.

"What the hell are you doing here?" I demand as Livia comes up behind me and shoves me out of the way to go barreling into his arms.

"Uncle Griffin!"

He scoops her up with ease and swings her around in circles on the front porch.

"Look at how big you've gotten. You're going to be taller than me soon," he tells her before setting her back down on her feet. "I told you we'd talk later, Kennedy. It's later."

Why? Why does he choose *now* to be a man of his word?

"Liv, why don't you go into your room and look through that new *Soldier of Fortune* magazine I got you?" I step aside so Griffin can come into the house, closing the door behind him. I'd really much rather slam the door in his face, but I'd never do that in front of Livia.

Griffin has always been amazing with my girls and they adore him. I feel a twinge of guilt over the fact that I shut him out of *their* lives as well. They've had a hard enough time dealing with the divorce ever since it was finalized a few weeks ago and their father being so self-absorbed that he can't even spend an hour with them every couple of weeks. Maybe I can try to be the bigger person here for their sakes.

Livia throws her arms around Griffin's waist and squeezes tight before racing off down the hall to her room.

"*Soldier of Fortune?*" Griffin asks me with a smile and a raise of his eyebrows.

"Oh, please. Don't act like that's a surprise. You're the one who bought her a camo bed set and all eleven seasons of *M*A*S*H* on DVD for her birthday last month," I remind him, my heart constricting at the fact that even during our estrangement he still remembered my daughter's birthday.

We stand there in the foyer staring at each other for a few minutes and the silence grows uncomfortable. Griffin and I have never been at a loss for words around each other. Even in the past when I've been irritated with him and his blatant, flirty comments or annoyed when he acts like a typical, self-absorbed guy, I had a lot to say.

This momentary truce I've declared in my head thirty seconds ago is already starting to mess with me. Standing here this close to him, I'm forgetting why I was even mad at him in the first place. Griffin moved to town after Alex and I had been dating for a few months, and suddenly I started to have doubts about my feelings for Alex. For a little while, it was a serious struggle for me to be around Griffin and not fantasize about being with him. To make matters worse, Griffin and Alex quickly became good friends and the three of us spent practically every waking moment together. He was sweet and thoughtful, even as a teenager, and he proved time and time again what a loyal friend he was to both of us.

A week before prom, Alex and I got into a typical teenage fight over something stupid and decided to take a break. Griffin, whom I'm assuming felt sorry for me, saved the day and told me he would be my date instead. I thought it was fate finally getting her shit together and deciding to join my side. Unfortunately, Griffin's ex-girlfriend at the time found out he asked me and she suddenly realized how much she loved him and begged him back. Griffin ditched me. Alex and I made up and the rest is history.

Or at least I thought. These past few days have been the first time I've been alone with Griffin since I dumped even the idea of Alex and me. It's the first time I've been single around him since high school and I'm suddenly reminded of all the reasons why I had such a huge crush on him back then. It's all I can do not to imagine him naked.

"So, are you ready to talk to me yet?" he asks, finally breaking the silence.

I take a step back from him and clear all thoughts of him in the buff from my head. It's making me twitchy.

"That depends. Are you going to try and feed me the same line of bullshit you did six months ago?" I ask as I cross my arms in front of me and stare him down.

He sighs deeply and runs his hand through his hair, making it stick up in all directions. He always does that when he's frustrated or angry. I wonder which it is right now. It's probably both.

"It wasn't bullshit, Kennedy. You only heard part of that conversation. I swear to you, I had no idea he was having an actual relationship with that woman."

I scoff at him and roll my eyes.

"Let's be honest here. She's not a woman; she's a child. A home-wrecking, slutty child and you condoned his behavior and told him to keep it from me," I tell him, trying to keep my voice down so the girls won't hear me.

"I should have never said that. At the time, I thought it was just a one-time thing. I thought he had just fucked up and it was never going to happen again. I knew it would kill you if you found out. And I didn't know you already had," he says.

He could be telling the truth. A part of me thinks it's kind of nice, albeit misguided, that he wanted to do what he could to save me from being hurt. But a bigger part of me has a hard time believing anything he says. The name of our business isn't Fool Me Once just for shits and giggles. I've lost my faith in mankind. Well, I've lost my faith in man, kind or not. Period.

"I haven't spoken to him at all since I found out the truth. I told him he was a lying sack of shit and a pathetic excuse for a man for doing that to you and the girls. He's tried calling me a bunch of times since then and I've ignored him. You know that you, Meadow, and Livia have always been my top priority."

At least that part isn't a lie; he's always made sure the girls and I are taken care of. Even with my giving him the cold shoulder and refusing to have anything to do with him the last six months, he's still called to talk to the girls and sent them gifts. And I know for a fact he's the one who hired a landscaper to mow my lawn every week, even though I know he won't admit it.

I always used to ask him why he never settled down and got married since I was sure he'd make an amazing husband and father. He would just shake his head and laugh and tell me that he'd get married when his dream girl became available. Then Alex would always pipe in about Griffin's celebrity crush—Megan Fox—and make a joke about her being too good for him.

"Well, the pathetic excuse for a man you speak of has gotten worse. He hasn't seen his daughters in two months. He was supposed to pick them up for dinner tonight and cancelled at the last minute. I'm sure Chloe with an *e* had episodes of *Sesame Street* she needed to watch or something." I try to make light of the situation. I can't take the heavy stuff right now. I can't handle thinking about how much I've missed having Griffin in my life.

"Chloe with an *e*? Am I missing something? Is there some other way you spell Chloe?" he asks with a laugh.

"He actually brought her to Uncle Wally and Aunt Janet's anniversary party a few months ago. He assumed that since he got an invitation before he cheated on me, he'd still be welcome. They stayed long enough for her to introduce herself. 'Like, hi everyone! I'm Chloe, with an *e!*'" I say in a singsong, squeaky voice. "Bobby and Ted dragged Alex outside and told him they would use him for target practice if he ever showed his face at one of our family get-togethers again with that whore."

Even though I wanted to puke when they walked into the restaurant together hand in hand, the night was made all better by watching Alex sob like a baby out in the parking lot. Real tears and everything. It was beautiful. If only he would have wet himself, I could have died a happy woman. Maybe next time.

"He's an asshole," Griffin growled.

"Yes, yes he is. Unfortunately though, there's nothing I can do about his assholishness. He's going to continue to let the girls down and all I can do is sit back and pick up the pieces," I tell him with a sigh. "Look, I don't want to talk about this anymore. All I want to think about right now is catching McFadden because he's really pissing me off. Thank you for saving my ass when he tried shooting at me. I appreciate it. But I work alone."

It's one thing to go easy on the guy so that he can still be in Meadow's and Livia's lives, it's a whole other thing to work side by side with him and try not to think about banging him. Or if he has birthmarks in any special places. Or tattoos that can only be seen with his pants off.

"I figured you'd say that. Which is why I came here tonight with a proposition for you," Griffin tells me, one side of his mouth tipping up into his signature grin.

I'm always a sucker for this man's smile and will agree to anything when he aims it in my direction. I should know by now just to run away when I see it.

"Fine. What's your proposition?" I ask.

Obviously, I'm a moron.

"How about a little wager? We'll each do our own separate thing. I didn't reenlist with the army and I'm on furlough from the police force right now because of budget cuts, so I need the work. But I'll leave you alone to chase after McFadden. If you catch him first, you win."

Who doesn't like a little bet? My heritage practically screams gambling aficionado; we go to the church and bet on simulcast horse racing all in the name of Jesus. If a Notre Dame game starts to get a little boring (don't tell my father I said that), we'll start placing bets on anything we can think of.

"I've got five on that super fan in the first row taking his shirt off before the third quarter."

"Double or nothing on the announcer saying the phrase 'ball and sack' in the same sentence by the end of the quarter."

"I'll wash your car for a week if there's a Budweiser commercial during the next break."

"What do I win, since we both know I'm going to get him first?" I ask with my own cocky smile.

"If you bring him in before I do, I'll let you get in one good solid punch to make up for the hurt I caused you," he replies.

Oh, man. He knows exactly how to sweet-talk a girl.

"Deal."

I quickly accept the bargain with a firm shake of his hand and as he's opening the front door to leave, my brain finally gets with the program and I realize I just agreed to this thing without asking what *he* would get if he caught McFadden first.

"Wait!" I shout to him as he gets to the bottom step and heads toward his motorcycle parked at the curb. "I know it's a long shot, but what do you win if *you* catch him first?"

Griffin grabs his helmet and after securing it on his head and swinging his leg to straddle the bike, he turns to look at me, and son of a bitch if I can't see the twinkle in his eyes through the visor of the helmet.

"If I win, you have to go on a date with me."

He starts up the bike with a roar of the engine and peels away from the curb, and I swear to God I can hear him laughing as he takes off down the street.

I walk back into the house with a slam of the front door and stand in my foyer cursing myself and my stupidity.

GD gambling problem.

CHAPTER 8

⌒

"Come on, ladies—harder! Faster!"

I hear a snicker from the corner of the exercise room at the fitness center and turn to see Paige thrusting her hips in the general direction of the heavy bag instead of punching it.

"Keep it up, McCarty, and you're going to run laps around the gym," I threaten her.

Paige gives me the finger and a sweet smile before turning back to the bag and punching it for all she's worth. I scan the rest of my class of about twenty women ranging in ages from sixteen to sixty and I smile at the progress they've made in the last few months. Most of them couldn't have hurt a fly when they walked in this room. Now, after a lot of hands-on instruction and some added kickboxing cardio, they can take down men twice their size.

I thought my Friday night self-defense class would be a good way to forget about Griffin's stupid proposal. Unfortunately, nothing is working in that department. I can't stop wondering if he's serious or not. And if he is serious, what the hell is he thinking? A date? With me? Is he out of his mind? First of all, we're friends. Or we used to be. And sort of are now, I guess. Or are we? Where the hell do we stand? I glance at the clock on the wall and realize it's five minutes past quitting time.

"All right, class, time's up. Great job. I'll see you all next week."

The sounds of twenty women hitting their heavy bags ceases and as they say their good-byes to each other and pack up their things, I walk over to Paige and Lorelei, who are sitting against the far wall chugging back water from their water bottles.

"Were you trying to kill us? I think my heart just exploded. Check my pulse." Paige thrusts her wrist out to me.

I stare at her in irritation. Even after an hour-long workout, she still looks perfect. Not one piece of hair is out of place and she hasn't even broken a sweat. Everyone else filing out of the room looks like they went ten rounds with Mike Tyson.

"How do you do that? How do you walk out of here looking exactly like you did when you walked in?" I demand as I take a seat across from them.

"It's a gift. Now, tell us why you kicked our asses tonight a hell of a lot harder than you normally do."

I sigh and start picking at the laces on my tennis shoes. "I made a bet with Griffin that if he catches McFadden before I do, I have to go on a date with him. Does that mean he asked me out on a date? I don't know. Probably not. Or did he? Sort of. I think."

Paige's face immediately takes on a far-off, happy look and she folds her hands neatly under her chin. "That is so romantic. What are you going to wear?"

I ignore her and turn to Lorelei, my voice of reason.

"You told him no, right?" she demands. "I mean, this is the jerk who never told you Alex was cheating on you. Is he insane? He's lucky you didn't kick him in the balls as soon as the words left his mouth."

I'm immediately bolstered by the fact that Lorelei used the word *balls* in a sentence and is on my side.

"That's what I'm sayin'," I reply, nodding my head in agreement.

"Oh, for the love of God. You two need to stop being Bitter Bettys. Not all men are jerks," Paige complains.

Lorelei and I stare at her in shock. Is she forgetting the name of our business and WHY we opened it in the first place? All men are most certainly jerks. The stacks of case files on our desks are living proof.

"What is wrong with you? How can you say that after what Andy did to you?" Lorelei questions her.

"Well, Andy should die in the fiery pits of hell and I think I'm allowed a little extra time to be bitter. You didn't see the black Louboutins I was denied from buying in Nordstrom that day. But I can still have hope for the future for my two best friends," Paige tells us.

"Well, good luck with that. I'm staying single forever. There is no man worth giving up my independence for," Lorelei says.

"Right there with you, sister," I agree as I put my fist up in the air to bump with hers and she just stares at it like it's going to bite her.

"You two are impossible. You're going to change your minds when you meet the right guy. And I'm pretty sure Kennedy here is going to be the first one eating her words. So, when's the big date and can I do your hair?"

I scoff at her and push myself up from the floor.

"I am not going on a date with Griffin Crawford."

Am I? No, no I'm not. It's insanity to even think that for a second.

But he's sweet, and good to your girls and every time you're around him all you can think about is taking his pants off.

SHUT UP, evil Kennedy!

He's an arrogant jerk who lied to your face and probably wouldn't hesitate to do it again.

Thank you, good Kennedy.

"Why did he even ask you out in the first place?" Lorelei questions as she and Paige follow me toward the exit.

"He didn't ask me out, remember? It's just a stupid bet. I guess. I don't know. I don't even know if he was serious," I complain. "I heard the word *bet* and all rational thought left the building."

As we walk to our cars, I explain to them in great detail about how he showed up at my house the previous night trying to plead his case and his parting words before he got on his bike and drove off into the night.

"Oh my God. You know what this means, right?" Lorelei presses the button on her key fob for her sleek, black Mercedes.

"That Kennedy and Griffin are going to go on this date, fall in love, and live happily ever after?" Paige tries, but can't hide the smile on her face.

"Will you pipe down with that shit?" I complain.

"No, it means that Griffin Crawford is going down," Lorelei states.

"Oooooh, that's hot," Paige coos.

Great. Now I have images of him naked with his face between my legs floating around in my head. This is not good. Not good at all.

"Get your mind out of the gutter, Paige," Lorelei scolds. "There are three of us and one of him. We are smart, resourceful, and good at what we do. If we can't catch that twit McFadden and you lose this bet, I will turn my back on everything I believe in and go out on a date myself."

Lorelei is right. Why the hell am I even worrying about the possibility of having to go on a date with Griffin? There is no way we're going to lose because we kick fucking ass.

"You guys will seriously help me do this?" I ask, pulling open my car door and throwing my bag into the passenger seat.

"Of course we will. That's what friends are for," Lorelei states matter-of-factly.

I turn to look at Paige and she stands there with her arms folded in silence until Lorelei finally smacks her shoulder.

"Ugggghhhh, fine! I'm in. But for the record, I still think you should just go on a regular date with the guy."

Ignoring her and the little butterflies in my stomach when I imagine what a date with Griffin would be like, I reach in and grab my cell phone out of the center console of my car and check my e-mail. When I see a fellow investigator's name at the top, I almost jump up and down in excitement.

"How would you girls feel about getting to work on winning this thing tonight? One of my contacts heard through the grapevine that McFadden is going to be trying to sell his alien hats at Mulligan's Bar and Grill tonight. If we hurry, we can make it there and catch this idiot. Someone's got to be drunk enough to buy one and stall him."

I glance up from my phone to see Lorelei with a huge smile on her face and Paige with an equally large frown.

"What now?" I ask her.

"We are not going out in public looking like this," she complains, spreading her arms out, indicating her attire.

"You look like you just stepped off the cover of *Vogue*," I fire back.

"Okay, fine. YOU aren't going out in public looking like *that*."

She points in the general vicinity of my hair, which is pulled up into a messy bun on the top of my head, and then down to my clothes, which include a pair of black nylon running shorts and a baggy, gray man's T-shirt with ARMY written in block letters across the chest.

"It's a college bar. Who gives a shit what I'm wearing?" I complain.

"*I* give a shit what you're wearing. And so would McFadden—you'll stick out like a sore thumb. As your friend, I cannot allow you to do this to yourself," Paige replies.

"We don't have time for this. If we don't hurry, we might miss him. I am NOT losing this bet."

Paige walks around to the back end of her red VW Bug convertible and opens the trunk.

"Lucky for you, I always come prepared," she tells me, pulling out three garment bags and a makeup case the size of a suitcase. "Both of you hightail it back inside to the showers. I'll have the two of you runway ready in less than twenty minutes."

Lorelei doesn't put up an ounce of complaint as she turns and hustles back toward the building. Lorelei is always up for one of Paige's makeovers.

"I don't need to be runway ready. I need to be ass-kicking ready," I argue.

"Are you seriously questioning my ability to do both? It's like you don't even know me, Kennedy O'Brien. That cuts me deep," Paige says with a sigh and a pout.

Looking at the time on my cell phone, I mutter and curse to myself as I throw my hands up in the air in defeat and trudge along behind Lorelei. There's no point in arguing with Paige; she will always win. And honestly, there's a reason why she is the master at catching cheating spouses: she always looks gorgeous, she's resourceful, and she never takes no for an answer.

GD model and her guilt trips.

CHAPTER 9

❧

I don't see him yet, do you?" Paige asks as she scans the crowded bar.

"I can't see anything through all this fucking mascara," I complain as I blink my heavy eyelids and look around the packed room.

"Oh, quit your bitching. You look amazing," Paige replies as she rests an elbow on the edge of the bar and signals the bartender.

Looking down at myself, I must agree. After Lorelei and I took the fastest showers ever, Paige unzipped the first garment bag and pulled out a black, pleated dominatrix-style bustier with a zipper down the front and two black buckles across the waist and a pair of skinny Seven jeans. It was badass and it was totally me. Unfortunately, it was also totally Paige's size since the clothes she keeps stocked in her car are for her assignments.

As I didn't have enough time to do anything other than throw on the ill-fitting clothes and hop into the car, Paige jury-rigged my outfit while I drove with a few well-placed safety pins, double-sided tape, and a sewing kit. A pair of tall, pointy-toed matching black boots with buckles on the sides completed the outfit and once they were on and Paige disappeared under the steering wheel while I was stopped at a red light to cuff the bottom of the jeans, you couldn't even tell they were a mile too long for me.

I might keep the jeans to replace the ones I ruined during my and Griffin's roll in the grass. Not to be confused with roll in the hay. Even though sometimes I think I *want* to be confused with a roll in the hay. With Griffin. Naked. In a bed. Or against a wall. Or on a kitchen table.

Shit!

"Could you order me a white wine spritzer, please?" Lorelei asks as she moves to my other side and perches on the edge of a bar stool, wiping the edge of the bar down with a wet wipe before placing her folded hands there.

As Lorelei scrunches up her nose at the bartender when he tosses down a bowl of peanuts in front of her that spill everywhere, I take in her usual work outfit—a cream, formfitting silk button-down blouse, black straight-leg dress pants, and black patent-leather Mary Janes and I have to admit, Paige really is a genius. Not because she had a perfect Lorelei outfit in her bag, but because she backed down when Lorelei threatened to have her committed if she tried to dress her in a red leather minidress and matching thigh-high stiletto boots.

"Sweetie, this is a dive bar. They probably don't even know what wine is," Paige informs her with a laugh.

"I'm confused. Why would this McFadden guy even come to a place like this? It's a college bar. It doesn't seem like his scene," Lorelei questions as she looks around.

"Supposedly, he comes here all the time to try and recruit college kids for his cause. I guess drunk twentysomethings must be easy to fool into believing that aliens exist," I explain as I tug the front of my bustier up a little higher so I'm not arrested for indecent exposure.

"Or drunk twentysomethings are easy to put foil hats on and convince to prance around the bar," Paige adds.

"That too."

"Oh my God. Oh no. Oh. My. GOD," Lorelei whispers as she stares with wide eyes at something over my shoulder.

"Really, it's not that bad. Just get a rum and Coke or something," Paige says with a roll of her eyes as she digs in her clutch and pulls out a tube of lip gloss.

"Turn around. Wait, no. Don't turn around. Oh my God. Okay, turn around really slowly but act natural," Lorelei tells us in a voice filled with panic.

Paige and I completely ignore her instructions and quickly turn around at the same time.

The blood drains from my face and the noise from the bar suddenly disappears. Across the bar, right by the door, standing arm in arm with a gaggle of girlfriends, is Chloe with an *e*. I'm now even more appreciative of Paige and her decision to pretty me up before we left the gym. It's bad enough that this bitch is thirteen years younger than me, but she also looks like Malibu Barbie with long, straight blonde hair, a spray tan, and fake boobs that are so high up on her chest she could rest her chin on them.

"Here, drink this," Paige orders as she holds a shot glass full of amber liquid in front of me.

Without taking my eyes off Hussy the Home Wrecker, I grab the glass and down the shot, letting the fiery burn make its way down my throat and into my stomach. Handing the glass back to Paige, I demand another one and she puts her fingers in her mouth and whistles for the bartender.

"Someone needs to give that woman a cheeseburger. She looks like she hasn't had a good, solid meal since birth," Lorelei states as she gets up off her bar stool and links her arm through mine.

"She needs to be waterboarded with pasta and potatoes," Paige agrees as she hands me another shot.

This one doesn't burn as it goes down and I'm starting to feel a little better about the fact that I'm in a bar with my ex-husband's mistress a few feet away and she looks like a porn star.

"It's okay. I'm fine. Totally fine. No big deal," I mutter to myself as another shot is placed into my hand.

"I think that's enough shots," Lorelei tells Paige as some of the alcohol misses my mouth when I tip the glass back and it dribbles down my chin.

"A little tequila is good for the soul," Paige replies as she pulls a tissue out of her purse and wipes my chin.

The alcohol is starting to kick in and the liquid courage is flowing through my veins. Who cares if she looks like Pamela Anderson and is half my age? Who cares if she can put both her feet behind her head and is so skinny that when she turns sideways she disappears? Not me. I could kick her ass with no arms or legs. I could kick her ass with LORELEI's arms and legs. I could kick her ass with my newly highlighted hair while swinging Lorelei's arms and legs over my head.

I think I'm drunk.

"Maybe you should take her gun away from her," I hear Lorelei mutter right next to me.

Just when I think my courage is off the charts, Harlot Barbie turns in my direction and we make eye contact. It could be the jukebox in the corner of the bar messing with me, or it could be the tequila, but I'm pretty sure I just heard the whistling tune of the gun-duel music that plays in old westerns.

The crowd parts like the Red Sea as she smiles and starts walking in my direction. Barbie's sidekicks, Skipper and Stacie, follow closely behind her until she stops a foot away from me and they both bump into her back, sending them all stumbling forward in a mess of blonde hair and fake boobs.

"Oh sweet Jesus," Paige mutters next to me.

"Kennedy! It's so good to see you! These are my friends, Misty, with a *y* and Tiffanie with an *ie*," Chloe says brightly.

"My IQ just dropped a hundred points," Lorelei whispers into my ear.

Suddenly, standing this close to the woman who stole my husband, I don't feel so good about myself. I can actually feel the tequila churning in my stomach and my awesome hair that Paige styled wilting into an ugly mess.

"How have you been? I feel like we haven't talked in ages," Chloe says with a pout of her perfect collagen-injected, bright pink lips.

Is this bitch serious? She's acting like we're old friends and not like I walked into my home to find her deep-throating my husband on my couch. MY couch. The brown leather piece of perfection I got on sale before I left for Afghanistan. I had to bleach the couch two days later. And then it was completely ruined. I miss that couch.

I can't even find my voice to tell her off. I've dreamed of this moment for months: coming face-to-face with my archnemesis in a bar with my friends, full of booze and looking awesome, and telling her exactly what I think of her while pummeling her face into a pile of wet dog food.

Instead, *I* feel like a pile of wet dog food. Wet dog food covered in shit and stuck to the bottom of someone's shoe. I feel inadequate. I never feel inadequate. I never care what people think of me, but right now I feel sorry for myself and I want to go off into the corner and cry into an entire bottle of tequila.

Before I can cede my title of awesomeness to the better woman, I feel warm hands grab onto my hips and then slide around to my front, pulling me back against a rock-hard chest. I see Chloe, Misty, and Tiffanie's eyes widen and their mouths drop open as fingers graze my bare shoulder and push my hair to the side before soft lips are pressed to my neck.

"Hello, gorgeous. Sorry I'm late. Traffic was a bitch."

I close my eyes as Griffin's voice rasps right by my ear, just loud enough for everyone in my general vicinity to hear. Without thinking, I turn in his arms and rest my hands against his chest. The corner of his mouth tips up in a mischievous grin as he stares into my eyes. One of his hands comes up and grabs onto the back of my neck, his other hand slides down to my ass and he pulls me roughly up against him. Without even sparing a glance to the three women behind me, his head swoops down and he crashes his lips against mine.

My brain shorts out and I can practically hear the crackling of electricity in my head when his tongue slides against my lips and I instinctively open my mouth to him. His tongue slides achingly slow against my own as he deepens the kiss and everything around me disappears. I tightly grab on to chunks of his hair on the back of his head to hold him in place as he tilts his head to the side to get a better angle.

Jesus, God, this man can kiss.

I raise myself up onto my toes and wrap my arms fully around his neck so I can press as close to him as possible while his mouth works slowly against my own. As his tongue continues to swirl around mine, I feel a tingle shoot through my body and it makes me want to wrap my legs around his hips and slide myself against the hardness I can feel pressed against my lower stomach.

Somewhere in the back of my mind I hear Lorelei clear her throat loudly and Griffin slows down the kiss, ending it with a few soft pecks on my swollen lips before pulling his head back to stare down at me.

"Ummmm, so what's new with you?" I hear Chloe ask from somewhere to my right.

"Sorry to be so rude, but Kennedy can't talk right now," Griffin responds without taking his eyes off my face. Normally I would protest when a guy speaks for me, but he's right. I can't talk right now. I can't even feel my legs. Do I still have legs? What day is it?

He continues to stare directly at my lips as he removes his hand from my ass and reaches into his back pocket, pulling out his wallet and extending his arm out in Paige and Lorelei's general direction. "Next round of drinks is on me. If you ladies will excuse us, Kennedy and I are going to find a quiet corner where we can be alone."

Out of the corner of my eye I see Paige grab Griffin's wallet. He slides his palm up my arm and pulls one of my hands down from around his neck, entwining our fingers together and then pulling me away from the girls. I follow blindly behind him, not giving a crap where he's taking me, as long as we can do some more kissing. When we make it far enough away from everyone, he turns to me and lets go of my hand.

"Sorry about that. It looked like you needed a little rescuing."

The euphoria from the kiss leaves me with a *whoosh* and now all I can think about is punching the mouth that was attached to mine moments ago. He didn't kiss me because he wanted to; he kissed me because he felt like he needed to. I don't give a shit that his performance was top-notch and that I can feel Chloe and her friends' eyes boring holes in the back of my head with their envy; all I care about is the fact that I was ready to mount him in the middle of a crowded bar and he just did it for show.

"I don't need anyone to rescue me. Especially you," I growl at him before turning and walking toward the door.

GD lack of self-control.

CHAPTER 10

After a restless night of tossing and turning, where I spent most of my time thinking about kissing Griffin again instead of punching him in the face, I get even more pissed off when I look in my cupboard and realize I don't have any coffee.

I swear to God the universe hates me.

At least today is football day. Football cures everything. Even smug, arrogant bastards who give you the best kiss of your life and then act like it was no big deal. Walking over to my slow cooker, I check on the status of my Buffalo Wing Dip that I always make for game day. I'm not much of a cook, but I can throw together a mean Buffalo Wing Dip.

"Mom, can you take me to the mall? I have nothing to wear to Grandpa's."

Turning around, I see Meadow standing in the kitchen naked.

Okay, not naked, but close enough.

"What the hell are you wearing?" I ask her in shock as I take in one of the Aéropostale T-shirts I bought her before school started. If you can still call it a T-shirt. It looks like she took a pair of rusty scissors to it and hacked off 90 percent of the material. The sleeves are missing now and the only thing left is the word *Aero*, which barely covers the boobs she just started growing and leaves her stomach and torso on full display. And now that she's sprouted up and is almost as tall as I am, she's decided to confiscate a pair of my Seven jeans, which are riding so low on her hips that if I squint, I can probably see Meadow's meadow.

Oh, hell, no.

"These are called clothes, Mom," she tells me in an exasperated voice with a roll of her eyes.

"You look like a streetwalker. And not even a high-priced one at that. You aren't going anywhere until you put *more* clothes on. Preferably a turtleneck. And thermal underwear," I tell her as calmly as I can with clenched teeth.

"You are being unreasonable!" she argues with a stomp of her foot.

"I know. I'm the worst mother in the world and all your friends' mothers are cooler than me and let their daughters dress like hookers," I inform her as she lets out a growl of frustration, turns, and stomps out of the room.

"You'll thank me one day when they're all working at McDonald's and you're a doctor!" I yell to her.

If this is what she's like *before* she gets her period, I'm moving out when that day happens. Or shipping her to a convent to let the nuns handle her.

As I leave the kitchen to go check on Livia and see if she's ready to go, I'm stopped in the living room by the ringing of the doorbell. Looking through the peephole, I let out a gasp when I see who it is.

"Alex, what are you doing here?" I ask my ex-husband when I open the door to him.

I haven't seen him in months. The only communication we've had is through text. For a minute I freak out, wondering if Chloe went home last night and told him about the kiss to end all kisses. He's wearing a tight-fitting green Hollister T-shirt, a pair of skinny jeans, and black Chucks. He looks like a teenager. Or like he's having a midlife crisis, which I'm guessing is what happens when you date someone half your age.

"Hi, Kennedy. You're looking good," he tells me with a smile. "I thought I'd stop by and see if I could take the girls today. I feel awful that I've been so busy lately and haven't had time to spend with them."

To say I'm shocked by his sudden interest in our daughters is an understatement. But then I get a good look at his face and see a black-and-purple bruise discoloring one eye and my mouth drops open. Seeing him with a goatee AND a soul patch is disturbing enough, but seeing him with a black eye is downright unnerving.

"What the hell happened to your face?"

I watch as his cheeks turn pink from embarrassment and he reaches one hand up to touch the bruise.

"Oh, this?" he asks with an uncomfortable chuckle. "I ran into a door. No big deal. So, can I take the girls?"

He's lying. He's totally lying. I am quite familiar now with the way he acts when he lies. Before I can question him further, he looks over my shoulder and one of his eyebrows rises questioningly.

"Hi, baby. What in the world are you wearing?"

I turn around, expecting to see Meadow standing behind me in her slut-wear and am pleasantly surprised when I see she took my advice. A little to the extreme though when I see she has on a turtleneck, hooded sweatshirt, drawstring sweatpants, Ugg boots, a scarf, and gloves. I'm sure she thought that by doing this it would make me feel bad, but this child doesn't realize she's dealing with the master.

"Mom told me to get dressed. I'm dressed. Are you happy now?" she asks, turning an angry glare in my direction.

"Perfectly," I reply with a big smile on my face. "Go get your sister—your father wants to spend the day with you guys."

Meadow's face immediately loses the preteen irritation and she looks at Alex hopefully. "Can we go to the mall?!"

Alex looks back and forth between Meadow and me uncomfortably and stutters his response. "Uh . . . um . . . well . . ."

"Your dad would LOVE to take you to the mall!" I say in an excited voice.

Let *him* deal with her attitude when she wants to shop at Sluts "R" Us and he vetoes it. At least he better veto it. Considering whom he's dating, he probably has a frequent-shopper card for every whorish store in the mall.

Meadow turns and runs excitedly down the hall, yelling for Livia and leaves me alone with Alex again.

"So, how have you been? Are you seeing anyone?" Alex asks.

Geez, nothing like getting right to the point.

"Oh, you know . . ." I trail off with a shrug.

DOES he know? Did Chloe fill him in on all the details? The way Griffin only had eyes for me, his hand on my ass, how tightly he held me against him, the slow way he worked me over with his lips and tongue?

Jesus, it's hot in here.

"Chloe said she saw you at the bar last night with her girl-friends."

Shit. He knows. Am I happy he knows? Maybe he's jealous. Good. This asshole needs to be jealous. He needs to be burning with rage that I made out with his ex–best friend.

"Oh, that's right! I totally forgot we ran into her."

Lies, lies, lies.

Come on, ask me about Griffin. Ask me about kissing him so I can rub it in your stupid face.

"She said you guys had a good time together."

What the fuck? The only good time had by the two of us would be in a boxing ring.

"I'm really glad you can be the bigger person, Kennedy. I don't know if I would be able to do the same thing if I were in your shoes," he tells me.

You ARE in my shoes, you asshole! I kissed Griffin! Just admit that you know and that you hate it!

"DADDY!" Livia comes running into the living room and throws herself in his arms.

"Hi, princess! I've missed you so much," he tells her as she wraps her legs around him and he holds her in his arms.

"Are you taking us to the mall? Can we go to Claire's so I can buy some new earrings and bracelets and then go to the pet shop so I can cuddle the puppies?" she asks sweetly.

Alex and I both stare at her in confusion for a few minutes before she laughs at both of us.

"Just kidding! I want to go to the sporting goods store and check out the new crossbows they just got in," she informs him as he leans over and sets her down on her feet.

"Okay, I'm ready to go," Meadow states as she joins us in the living room. She's removed all of her winter wear and put my Seven jeans back on, but at least she's now wearing a shirt that actually covers her body. And decided to add a thick protective layer of makeup.

"Uh, is she allowed to wear makeup?" Alex asks me.

"Good luck with that," I tell him as I lean over and kiss each of the girls good-bye. I've had to parent them on my own for months now. It's his turn.

As soon as they are out the door, I grab my pot of Buffalo Wing Dip and take it out to my car, securing it in the backseat before pulling out and heading to my father's house. When I reach his cul-de-sac, my annoyance over the fact that Alex never once mentioned what happened between Griffin and me last night disappears. The street has been blocked off and is filled with my father's neighbors, all wearing the signature blue-and-gold colors of Notre Dame. I'm pretty sure when they bought this house when my mom was pregnant with Ted, they made it a requirement of the Realtor to find them a house in Notre Dame territory. In the street there are picnic tables, cafeteria tables, and chairs, and enough food to feed an army. Or a herd of football fans. As I slowly pull into my father's driveway, I see that he and my brothers have brought out his big-screen television and set it in the front yard with an extension cord. Today is going to be a good day.

Grabbing the Crock-Pot from the backseat, I make my way down the driveway and over to one of the tables where I see my father, Aunt Janet, and Uncle Wally.

"Is that Buffalo Wing Dip? It better be Buffalo Wing Dip," Dad tells me as he eyes the Crock-Pot in the crook of my arm.

I haven't spoken to my dad since I found out Griffin is the guy he hired, and refusing him his favorite football game snack is a good way to tell him I'm pissed at him about it. I set the Crock-Pot down at the far end of the table, out of his reach.

"Did you put in an extra cup of cheddar cheese?" he asks, staring at the Crock-Pot instead of me.

"I put in *two* extra cups of cheddar cheese. But you're not getting any of it," I threaten.

"Awwwww, come on, Kennedy. I'm an old man. Don't deny me my Buffalo Wing Dip," he complains, licking his lips as he watches Uncle Wally lift the lid and take a big whiff.

"Put that lid back on, Uncle Wally," I scold, not taking my eyes off my father.

"What did I do?" Uncle Wally whines.

"Both of you know damn well what you did. Anyone care to tell me why they felt the need to hire Griffin to help me on your bail-jumping case?" I ask, crossing my arms in front of me and tapping my foot.

Aunt Janet pipes up. "Griffin? I haven't talked to him in a few weeks. How is he?"

"You're not helping," I tell her through clenched teeth.

"Oh, what's the big deal? I needed extra help and Griffin needed work," my dad says with a shrug as he slides down the bench seat and reaches for the Crock-Pot lid.

"The big deal?" I argue, smacking his hand away as he gives me a dirty look. "The big deal is that I can't work with him. He's cocky and manipulative and annoying."

"You're forgetting handsome, persistent, and a great kisser."

I jump in surprise and a squeak flies out of my mouth when I hear Griffin's voice behind me.

"Kennedy, you kissed Griffin?" Aunt Janet asks excitedly.

"Technically, I kissed her. But she was an equal participant," Griffin replies.

I hear my aunt mutter, "It's about time," under her breath and I turn around to give him a scathing look for airing this dirty laundry in front of my family. As soon as I look at him though, I'm reminded of that stupid kiss and dammit if I don't want to haul him off behind the bushes and do it again.

"So are you guys dating now?" my father asks with a smile as he quickly shovels in a few mouthfuls of dip.

Turning away from Griffin's smiling face, I take a page out of Meadow's handbook and stomp angrily over to the end of the table. I slam the lid back down on the Crock-Pot, narrowly missing my father's fingers.

"Heeeeeeey!" he complains as I snatch the Crock-Pot up from the table and shove it under my arm.

"NO DIP FOR YOU!" I whirl around and storm toward the house.

"If you guys are dating now, you can just split the finder's fee on McFadden, right?" Uncle Wally shouts to me.

I hear Griffin's chuckle as I throw open the door to my father's house and go inside.

GD family.

CHAPTER 11

$\mathcal{C}\!\!\!\sim\!\!\!\sim$

I pace angrily back and forth in my father's kitchen, muttering to myself.

"Stupid man and his stupid infuriating grin. Stupid family. Stupid me for thinking about that damn kiss . . ."

"Can we talk, or do you need a minute?" Griffin asks as I turn and see him lounging against the doorway with a smile on his face.

"Why are you here?"

He pushes off the wall and walks over to me in the middle of the kitchen. Reaching up with one hand, he brushes a strand of hair out of my eyes with his fingertips and I have to fight the urge not to shiver when his fingers graze the skin of my forehead. I notice something out of the corner of my eye though and I grab his hand and hold it in front of my face.

"Why are your knuckles bruised?" I demand as I stare at the red, swollen area and lightly run my thumb over it.

He shrugs and pulls his hand out of my grasp. "Oh, you know. Ran into a door or something. I don't remember."

It occurs to me that Alex gave me the same answer when I asked him what happened to his face.

"Griffin, what did you do?" I demand.

"Don't worry about it," he answers quickly.

Oh my God. He punched Alex in the face. Why did he punch Alex in the face now? I told him the other night about Alex being a deadbeat dad and then this morning, Alex suddenly shows up at my house with a shiner, wanting to spend time with the girls. Did he seriously go to Alex's apartment and beat him up for me? For the girls? This should piss me off. Alex should *want* to spend time with his own daughters without needing his face rearranged to do it. It doesn't piss me off though; it melts my frozen heart.

"Griffin," I whisper softly, looking up into his face.

"Did he pick the girls up?" he asks.

I nod in response, unable to speak.

"Good."

He brings his hand up and cups my cheek in his palm, rubbing his thumb slowly back and forth against the side of my face, staring at my mouth. I feel my insides melting into a puddle of goo and I want him to kiss me so badly I feel like I'm going to scream if he doesn't do it already.

As he eases his head down to me, I start to close my eyes in anticipation of his lips against mine. Then, my stupid brain has to interfere and I remember what happened last night. It was all fun and games until the kiss was over.

Putting both of my hands flat against his chest, I shove him away angrily and take a few steps back.

"No. No, no, no. You don't get to kiss me again. Not after that crap last night," I tell him angrily.

"Crap? I thought that kiss was pretty amazing. Crap? Really?" he asks again in shock.

How can a man this good-looking be so dense?

"*I thought you needed rescuing,*" I say in a mocking voice, just like his the previous night. "I don't need you, or anyone to rescue me. And I definitely don't need you or any man to kiss me because he feels sorry for me."

I watch as the lightbulb finally clicks on and the humor in his eyes gets replaced by something fierce as he stalks toward me. I quickly move backward until I bump up against the counter and have nowhere else to go. Griffin puts his arms on either side of me on the counter, caging me in.

"Let's get something straight here," he tells me with a firm voice. "I have never felt sorry for you. When I kiss you, it's because I want to, not because I have to. I saw the look on your face last night. You felt like shit next to that girl. You're too much of a stubborn hard-ass to feel like less than you are around anyone. Especially someone like her."

His eyes bore into mine and butterflies flap manically around in my stomach. Why is it so hard to stay mad at this man?

Without giving it a second thought, I grab the front of his shirt with both of my fists and haul him toward me, crashing my lips against his. Right now, I don't care how bad of an idea this is. No one has ever said anything like that to me before and meant it.

Griffin immediately pushes his tongue past my lips and I moan into his mouth when I taste him again. He grabs onto my hips and effortlessly lifts me up onto the counter. My legs immediately wrap around his waist and my hands fist in his hair as he swirls his tongue through my mouth and pushes his hips between my legs. I can feel his erection again, just like last night, but this time, the hardness of him is right where I want it, pushing against the ache that formed as soon as he spoke those words to me. His hands slide around to my ass and he pulls me closer to the edge of the counter. I instinctively thrust my hips against him and it's his turn to groan.

It's been far too long since I've felt this needy. Every inch of my body is on fire and I can't stop pushing my body against him. Jesus, he feels so good between my legs, sliding himself against me. I'm ashamed to admit that if he keeps this up, I'm probably going to have the fastest orgasm known to man. Or woman. His lips leave mine and he makes a trail of kisses across my cheek and to the side of my neck as he grips my ass and moves me against him. The tip of his tongue traces the edge of my earlobe before he tugs on it gently with his teeth.

"Fuck, you taste good. I've wanted you like this for eighteen years," he murmurs, pressing a kiss to my neck.

Whoa. The fuck?

My hands, which are still locked in a death grip in his hair, tighten hard enough to pull some strands out as I yank his head away from my neck and stare angrily in his eyes.

"What did you just say?"

He tries to move back toward my lips, but I stop him, pulling on his hair even harder until he yelps. "Ouch! Easy on the hair!"

"Tell me you did not just say what I think you said!"

Griffin sighs and bows his head.

Holy shit. He's serious. How did I not know this? And why the hell am I just finding out about this NOW? I thought the whole "go on a date with me" thing was just to bait me. Why the hell am I suddenly regretting all of the years I wasted with Alex when I could have had Griffin? SHIT! NO! He's a friend. A friend who can kiss like a god and almost make me come on my father's kitchen counter. We need to talk about this. This is serious business. I'm not ready for serious business. Why am I even questioning myself?

"So I guess this means you ARE dating?" my father asks from the kitchen doorway.

"GAAAAAAAAH!" I scream in frustration as I push Griffin away and jump down off the counter.

"Yes," Griffin replies calmly.

"We most certainly are NOT dating!" I yell at Griffin.

"Just a matter of time until I catch McFadden," he tells me with a grin.

"I'm going to wipe that smile off your face when *I* catch him and punch you square in the mouth!" I shout back.

"I don't know what's going on here, and I don't care. I just came in to get the dip," my father replies with a longing look toward the Crock-Pot resting on the counter right next to where I had been close to orgasm. Griffin wanted me for eighteen years and never said a word about it until now.

SHIT!

"Am I interrupting something?" Paige asks as she enters the kitchen and sees all of us standing here.

"NO!"

"Yes," Griffin and I state again at the same time, causing me to growl in frustration.

"I think they're dating. I just want my dip. Tell her to give me my dip, Paige," my dad whines.

"Did you lose the bet?" Paige asks me in confusion.

"What bet?" Dad asks.

"Griffin bet Kennedy that if he finds McFadden first, she has to go on a date with him," Paige informs him.

"I've got ten on Griffin," Dad tells her, reaching for his wallet.

"DAD!"

Griffin laughs as he leans against the counter and folds his arms in front of him.

"I'll take that bet, and raise you twenty," Paige replies.

At least someone is on my side.

"Kennedy, do you have your gun on you?" she asks as she pulls her purse off her shoulder and starts digging through it.

"Uh, yeah. Why?"

Paige finds her wallet and counts out thirty dollars, slapping it down on the kitchen table.

"Because, McFadden is outside flipping burgers three houses down."

Griffin pushes away from the counter and his arms fall to his sides. We look at each other in silence for five seconds before we both take off at a dead run out of the kitchen, shoving Paige and my father out of the way.

"You could have led with that, you know!" I yell at Paige as I race to the front door.

"This was more fun!" she shouts back as Griffin and I fight over the door handle, pushing and shoving each other out of the way. Griffin slams his hip into mine and I stumble backward as he flings open the front door, sprinting outside into the sunshine. I take off after him while I curse Paige. She could have pulled me aside and told me about McFadden quietly.

GD lack of loyalty.

CHAPTER 12

~~~

I race down the front porch just in time to see Griffin standing in the middle of the yard looking left to right, trying to decide which direction to run. My dad's house is right smack in the middle of the cul-de-sac. There are seven houses on either side of his house, each one filled with people getting ready to root on Notre Dame. I need to pick the right direction. WHICH ONE IS THE RIGHT DIRECTION?!

Looking to my left, I see that Lorelei just arrived. And she's wearing a maroon-and-gold silk blouse with matching maroon dress pants: Arizona Sun Devils' colors, the team that Notre Dame is playing today. She's going to be killed!

I see her lift her arm and point in the opposite direction that Griffin is currently looking and send her a thumbs-up before sprinting away. She's on her own; I can't save her from crazy Notre Dame fans now.

Running at top speed and yelling for people to get out of my way, I make it to the Andersons' house, three houses down, in record time.

"Where's the grill?" I ask the first person I come to through gasps of air.

"The burgers aren't done yet," a guy with a giant navy-blue foam finger tells me as he uses the foam finger to scratch his nose.

71

"WHERE'S THE FUCKING GRILL?!" I scream at him, pulling my gun out of the holster under the back of my shirt.

He doesn't even bat an eye when he sees the 9mm in my hand. Half of the people on this street carry guns. Football season is serious business. Plus, most of the people here know that my family all works in some sort of law enforcement.

"If you're that hungry, I heard someone brought Buffalo Wing Dip a few houses down." He points his foam finger back in the direction I came.

"There's a criminal cooking burgers on your grill. Where is the grill?" I ask again as I check the safety on my gun.

"Bob Anderson is a criminal? Damn, it's always the quiet ones," foam-finger guy states with a sad shake of his head.

I'm going to take his foam finger and shove it up his ass in three seconds.

"No, not Bob Anderson. His name is Martin, he skipped bail, and rumor has it he's manning the grill at this house," I tell him through clenched teeth.

"You mean McFadden? I just met him. Nice guy. And he has a cute dog."

Sweet mother of God . . .

"The grill's around back," he tells me with another point of his finger. "Don't shoot the dog!"

Looking over my shoulder to make sure Griffin isn't anywhere in sight, I take off running again, keeping myself pressed to the side of the house as I move quickly with my gun in front of me. Peeking around the back corner, I see the grill about ten yards away from the house. And I see McFadden with his back to me, all alone with Tinkerdoodle sitting by his feet staring up at him, hoping one of the burgers he's flipping drops on the ground.

Edging out from around the side of the house, I hold my gun out in front of me and creep closer, careful not to make a sound.

When I'm within three feet of him, I check my back pocket to make sure the zip ties I usually carry are still back there, ready to be used when I tackle him and secure his hands behind his back.

"Hey, McFadden! Are those burgers almost done?"

I jump when I hear the yell from foam-finger asshole behind me and McFadden turns around from the grill with a giant spatula in his hand and a smile on his face. The smile dies when he sees me standing here with my gun pointed right at his chest.

"You can have the first burger. Just don't shoot me!" he says nervously.

"You are really pissing me off, Martin. Put the spatula down and let's do this calmly, without making a scene."

I can hear people talking behind me and roll my eyes when I realize the backyard is filling up with onlookers, wanting to see what's going on.

"Just because she brings a gun, she gets the first burger? I've been waiting for twenty minutes," someone whispers.

Michelle Anderson, Bob's wife, comes outside. "It's okay, everyone. That's Buddy's daughter, Kennedy. She's like that. Did Martin forget to bring a covered dish? I don't think you need to shoot him for that."

Can I just catch a break here? Seriously.

"Michelle, this man is a criminal. Can you please get everyone inside and out of danger?" I plead with her.

"This is so exciting. It's like an episode of *Cops*. Is someone filming this?" Michelle asks, completely ignoring my request as I move closer to McFadden.

Tinkerdoodle lets out a yippy bark and growls at me.

"It's okay, princess. She isn't going to shoot Daddy," McFadden tells the dog. "She's one of us. She believes in the 'others' and even bought one of Daddy's special hats."

While McFadden soothes the dog, I take another slow step in his direction and stop when the dog growls at me again.

"Put the spatula down and walk toward me slowly," I demand.

"Can't we just talk about this? I'll give you a signed copy of my book," he pleads.

Raising the gun higher, so it's aimed right at his face, I watch him swallow nervously and turn slowly to set the spatula down on the card table next to the grill, filled with buns and a huge cookie sheet of uncooked hamburger meat.

"Just so you know, I don't have any hard feelings toward you. We can still be friends after this is over," he states with his back still to me.

I take a deep breath and another cautious step in his direction, ignoring the growling dog by my feet with her teeth bared—her tiny little two-pound-dog teeth. I sort of want to laugh at the fact that this dog thinks she's some kind of badass guard dog.

When I'm within arm's reach, McFadden suddenly lets out a yell.

"TINKERDOODLE—ATTACK!"

The dog launches itself at my leg in a blur of activity and clamps down on my ankle. I let out a yelp as McFadden whirls around with the cookie sheet of meat in his hand and throws it in my direction. Raw meat rains down on my head while I try to keep the gun on McFadden and shake the stupid dog loose from my pant leg.

"Son of a bitch, that ground meat was $3.95 a pound!" Bob Anderson complains from somewhere in the yard.

Tinkerdoodle finally lets go of my ankle and races back to McFadden, who scoops her up in his arms and takes off running. I turn to go after him and my boot slips right through a slippery pile of ground meat. My feet fly out from under me and I land flat on my back, knocking the wind right out of me as I gasp for breath.

"SSSSSSSSSS—ssstooooop," I say through coughs as I turn my head to the side and see McFadden run right by the crowd of people who stand there. He stops and turns to look at me, holding his pinkie and thumb up to the side of his head and shouts, "Call me!" before taking off again.

"You've got meat in your hair," Bob Anderson tells me as he walks up next to me while I struggle to roll over, get up, and breathe at the same time.

Putting my hand to my chest, I try to take a deep breath and wind up coughing from the exertion. "Criminal. Stop. Can't. Breathe."

Bob looks down at me in confusion as I hack and try to breathe while moving as fast as I can to try to get up off the ground and chase after McFadden. Bob is retired from the police force and if anyone can understand what the hell is going on here, it will be Bob.

"McFadden? Nice guy. I just met him this morning. The missus met him at the grocery store and invited him."

"Bail. Jumper," I mumble between deep, heaving breaths that my lungs finally let me have and my hand squishes down into a pile of raw meat as I push myself up onto my knees.

"Really? Huh. He didn't look like a bail jumper," Bob states.

I am surrounded by idiots.

"What's with all the commotion? I heard the burgers are ruined," my dad says as he pushes through the crowd of onlookers and walks next to Bob, who finally gives me a hand and helps me up off the ground. I see McFadden's Honda go soaring down the street. With a sigh, I turn to my dad in irritation and see him standing there with a Styrofoam plate in his hand filled with my dip and tortilla chips.

"Really, Dad? You were just in the kitchen with me when Paige told us McFadden was here. You thought it was wise to stop for a snack instead of rushing to my aid?"

Dad shrugs as he shovels a chip full of dip into his mouth.

"I figured you had it under control. You know you have meat in your hair?"

"GOD DAMMIT!" I shout, with a stomp of my foot.

My dad's hand flashes out like lightening and smacks me on the back of the head, a chunk of meat coming loose and dropping down on the front of my shirt.

"T-minus five minutes until kickoff!" one of the neighbors shouts from a few feet away. Everyone in the yard, my father included, lets out a huge yell and they all disperse to head over to his yard where the TV is. The fact that they just witnessed a wanted man escape from a woman with a gun is of no concern to them now that it's game time.

With a scowl, I brush the globs of meat off my shirt and see Griffin pushing through the horde of people until he makes it to my side and tries to smother a laugh with his hand.

"Not a word. Not ONE word," I threaten him as I walk around him and shove my gun back in its holster.

"You have meat on your ass," he shouts to my back with a laugh.

GD meat-flinging McFadden.

CHAPTER 13

After rinsing all of the raw meat out of my hair and off my skin in my dad's shower, I step out, wrapping a towel securely around myself. I wipe the steam off the mirror with my hand and run a comb through my hair, pausing when there's a knock at the door. Figuring it's either Paige or Lorelei, I begin my tirade as I turn to open it.

"You know, a little help from my partners would have been nice when—"

The words die on my lips when I see Griffin standing there.

"I thought you didn't want to be partners. If you've changed your mind, just let me know," he says with a smile, as he looks me up and down. A shiver runs down my spine and it has nothing to do with all the heat from my shower rushing out the open door and everything to do with the way he's looking at me. Like he wants to lick all of the water off my skin.

"If you came up here to gloat, save your breath," I warn him, securing the towel tighter between my breasts, so it doesn't fall off.

Griffin doesn't say a word as he moves his large body into the small bathroom, forcing me to back up a few steps. With his eyes still locked on mine, I swallow thickly as he shuts the door behind him and turns the lock.

"I didn't come up here to gloat, I came up here to talk," he replies softly.

"I don't want to talk."

He shrugs nonchalantly, snaking one arm around my waist and pulling my towel-clad body roughly up against him. "That's an even better idea."

Before I can utter a protest, his mouth is on mine.

What is with this man? In the span of just a few days, he can't get enough of me.

One of his hands moves down to my ass and squeezes as his tongue slides past my lips and I forget all about the bet and the meat bath I just rolled in outside and kiss him back. He turns me and pushes my back up against the wall, his hand sliding down to my bare leg, pulling it up around his hip.

He's right; we really need to talk. About what he did to Alex, about the bet, about what the hell this thing is going on between us . . .

His palm slides up the back of my thigh until he's clutching my bare ass.

Okay, talking can wait.

"Keep your leg there," he demands softly against my lips.

I nod in acceptance, knowing full well that at this point, if he asked me to light my hair on fire, I would do it. My body is screaming for him to touch me, I don't care if there are a hundred people outside the house right now, I just want his fingers on me.

Shit! There are a hundred people outside right now and his hand is sliding off my ass and over my hip, heading right for the promised land, while he licks some droplets of water off my shoulder.

"Griffin, there are people outside," I moan as his fingers skim the inside of my thigh, inching closer and closer to where I want him.

"They're busy," he mumbles against the side of my neck as he kisses his way back up to my lips.

As if to punctuate his statement, I hear the crowd cheer outside right at the exact moment that the tips of his fingers graze between my legs with a featherlight touch.

First and ten.

I was wet for him as soon as he walked through the door and his fingers easily slide through my wetness and up to my clit, circling around it as the crowd goes wild again.

Forward pass.

He lets out a groan of desire when he feels how much I want him and finds my lips, sinking his tongue into my mouth at the same time one of his fingers pushes inside of me. I whimper into his mouth and wrap my arms tightly around his shoulders as his finger begins working slowly in and out of me. As I rock my hips against his hand, his finger pushes in deeper and the heel of his hand bumps against my clit each time I thrust forward. I feel myself losing control and my legs start to shake as I move faster and faster and his hand pushes in deeper and harder. He swallows all of my cries against his lips as I race to the edge. I can feel it building quickly as he works me over with his finger. I've never come this quickly in my life. I've never thrown caution to the wind and just let go. Everything I do is carefully thought out and planned. This is insanity. My orgasm is right there, just beyond my reach, but my brain is starting to interfere and I pull my mouth away from Griffin's, letting my head thump back against the wall with my eyes squeezed shut.

His hand stills with his finger pushed as far as it will go inside of me. I feel his lips against my ear a second later and his warm breath washes over me as his thumb circles around and around my clit, ever so gently.

I let out a gasp and a low moan when tingles of pleasure shoot through me once again and I buck my hips roughly against his hand.

"Let go, Kennedy, just let go," he whispers against my ear.

His thumb moves faster, back and forth, bringing me right back to the edge and when I feel him curl his finger inside of me,

I tumble over, clutching him against me as I cry out through my release and the crowd outside once again starts cheering.

Touchdown.

This is the orgasm to end all orgasms and I don't know if it's because it's Griffin who's giving it to me, because I'm doing something so out of character, or a little bit of both.

"Ride it out, baby," he tells me softly as another shout and round of applause is heard from out in the yard and he pushes a second finger inside me.

Two point conversion.

His fingers are stretching me and prolonging my orgasm until I feel like it's never going to end. I never *want* it to end and I continue to whimper and gasp as the waves of pleasure just keep coming and coming.

I can't catch my breath and I don't even care. My hips keep moving and his fingers keep pumping inside of me until the pleasure eventually trickles away. Griffin kisses me softly on the lips as he pulls his fingers out of me and my leg falls limply from around his waist.

Holy Jesus. Who knew that coming along with a football game could be so amazing? More people should try this.

I feel his body move away from mine and I slowly open one eye to see him adjusting himself in his jeans.

I've never been much for blowjobs, but right now, there's nothing else I can think of except sinking down to my knees and taking him in my mouth.

"If you don't stop looking at me like that, I'm going to fuck you up against that wall," Griffin warns me.

I've also never been too keen on dirty talk, but thank God I'm not standing. My knees wouldn't have held me. I shift my gaze from his crotch to his face and see that he's completely serious. His hands are clenched into fists at his sides and it looks like it's taking everything in him not to rip my towel off me and make good on his threat.

Yes, please.

Without giving it a second thought, I reach up between my breasts and tug on the edge of the towel tucked there, causing the whole thing to fall off me and land at my feet on the floor.

"Oops," I whisper.

I watch as Griffin's mouth drops open and the bulge between his legs grows bigger.

He takes a step toward me right as the bathroom door bursts open and slams against the opposite wall, my brother Bobby standing there with a look of horror on his face. Bobby moved in with my dad after his last tour of duty so he could figure out what he wants to do with his life in between tours. Obviously he's now wishing he lived somewhere else.

I scream, Bobby screams, and Griffin dives to the ground to retrieve my towel, bringing it up in front of me and turning his back to give me cover.

"OH, JESUS, MY EYES! I CAN NEVER UNSEE THIS!" Bobby screams, covering his face with both of his hands, turning around and running blindly down the hall.

"BOBBY, WHAT THE HELL?" I yell. "The door was locked, you idiot!"

Securing the towel back around myself, I can feel my face heating up with embarrassment, all of the euphoria from moments ago long gone. There's a loud *"Ooof!"* that comes from the hallway followed by Lorelei's voice.

"Bobby, what are you doing? Take your hands off your eyes."

"The lock is broke. Oh, Jesus, the lock is broke. WHY, GOD, WHY?"

Lorelei peeks her head around the doorway and her eyes widen in surprise when she sees Griffin and me.

"Oh my," she mutters.

"Help," I manage to squeak out as I stare at her over Griffin's shoulder.

Lorelei's head disappears back into the hallway and I hear her console Bobby, who mumbles about how he can't make his feet move because he's blind.

"I think I'm going to be sick," Bobby whines from the hallway.

"In with the good air, out with the bad," Lorelei coaches him.

"Oh, for the love of God," I grumble. "Will you people just leave and go back outside!"

"Bobby! Where the hell is the beer?" I hear my dad yell up from the bottom of the stairs and then the unmistakable sound of him stomping up them.

Jesus. How about we just invite the whole damn neighborhood up here so they can see me half naked and post-orgasmic?

"What the hell happened to you?" I hear my dad ask Bobby from the stairway as Griffin turns around to face me.

"Things that can never be unseen. Bad things," Bobby mumbles.

I stare straight at Griffin's chest, refusing to look at him.

"Where's Kennedy? Is she done washing meat off herself yet? Quit blocking the hallway. I need her help," Dad complains.

"Kennedy and Griffin are in there . . . talking. They need to talk. You know, just talk. About . . . things," Lorelei explains to my father.

Great. Miss Powerhouse Attorney can't even form a coherent thought right now.

Bobby makes a gagging noise out in the hallway and if I were fully clothed right now I would go out there and kick his ass.

"Goddammit," Bobby moans, followed immediately by the sound of a *smack*, which I'm assuming is from my father's hand connecting with the back of Bobby's head.

"Griffin Crawford, you better be wearing protection while you talk to my daughter. Kennedy, we're out of dip and Steve Henderson just puked in the shrubs. Get dressed and come help," my dad yells before he stomps back down the steps.

"Come on, Bobby, let's get you some fresh air," Lorelei states as I hear her dragging him down the stairs.

When the front door slams shut a few seconds later, Griffin laughs and I finally glance up at him to give him a dirty look.

"This isn't funny," I hiss at him.

"It's pretty funny," he chuckles. "Can we cancel the bet and just tell everyone we're dating?"

Is he out of his mind? One orgasm does NOT equal dating. And the bet was HIS idea. I am seeing this shit through to the bitter end. I don't date. Especially not someone who throws out a line about wanting me for eighteen years in the middle of a make-out session. I don't want to date him, I don't want to fall in love with him, and I don't want him professing his stupid crush. I don't need this complication in my life. Thank you for the wonderful orgasm, but I'm done. Seacrest, out!

"We are NOT dating. And this bet isn't over until I win," I growl at him as I shoulder past him and out the door, my bare feet smacking angrily on the floor as I stomp across the hall to the spare bedroom and the extra clothes I keep there for emergencies.

"You should just concede now, Kennedy. You're never going to win!" Griffin yells to me as I walk into the bedroom and slam the door behind me.

GD cocky man and his mind-blowing orgasms.

CHAPTER 14

"Pour me a mother. I mean, pour me another," I slur as I hold my wine glass out to Lorelei and watch in fascination as the golden liquid splashes into my glass.

"It's so pretty," I whisper, bringing the glass to my mouth and taking a big sip.

It's Monday night, two days after the bathroom debacle. I spent the last two days looking up any and all information I could find on McFadden. Luckily, Alex decided to keep the girls for a few days so I've had the house all to myself. I spent every waking moment pouring over every single thing I could find on him from his elementary school grade cards to his most recent STD test. He sucked at math, but at least he doesn't have VD. I've been to every hangout he's ever been seen at and talked to every contact I have on the street and no one has seen him. I'm losing my touch. Why the hell is it suddenly so hard to find this tool? He's popped up where I've been twice and my informants have spotted him all over the place, but now, nothing. No one has seen or heard from him in two days. I am totally off my game and there is only one person to blame for that.

"Okay, so tell us again, in detail," Paige demands as she grabs the bottle of wine from Lorelei and tops off her own glass.

After not hearing from me for two days, the girls staged an intervention and showed up at my house this evening with enough wine to stock two shelves in my fridge. I'm not a wine drinker; I prefer beer. But since they were the ones buying, I couldn't be picky.

Why didn't anyone tell me wine is so delicious?

Tucking my feet under me on the couch, I feel myself start to sway back and forth and some of the wine from my glass sloshes onto my jeans.

"He has magical fingers, did I mention that part already?" I ask the girls.

"Yes, you've mentioned his magic digits several times. Get to the good part, for God's sake. Tell me you saw his penis," Paige demands.

"You don't have to answer that," Lorelei states firmly as she takes a sip of bottled water. Lorelei has a one-drink minimum. I've never seen her drunk. I think it's physically impossible for her to *get* drunk.

"She most certainly DOES have to answer that. I haven't seen a penis in months. I need to live vicariously through her," Paige argues.

"I did not have sexual relations with that man," I say in my best Bill Clinton voice. "I also did not get to see the peen."

Paige boos and hisses at my announcement and Lorelei rolls her eyes.

"Okay, so there's been a little bit of a setback with winning this bet. He's obviously trying to distract you with sex. We need to come up with a new plan of attack."

I blink a few times to get Lorelei's face into focus and see her sitting there tapping her finger against her lips while she thinks.

What if she's right? What if all of this was just a ruse to side-track me so *he* could take down McFadden? The kisses, the proclamation, the orgasm . . . it was all part of his evil master plan. I've been so flustered and distracted that I'm not thinking clearly and can't find a guy who should be easier to track down than this. It should have never taken me this long to catch a bail jumper.

SON OF A BITCH!

I jump up from the couch and throw my arms up in the air, forgetting the full glass of wine I still have in my hand as it spills all over the floor and coffee table and splashes on Paige's shoes.

"NOT MY JIMMY CHOOS!!!!" Paige screams.

Reaching for the wine bottle on the coffee table, I stick it right in front of her face. "Here, drink this and don't think about the shoes."

Paige sniffles and takes a sip of wine from her glass and then tips back the wine bottle and starts chugging.

"Oh my God, you do NOT chug a one-hundred-and-fifty-dollar bottle of Domaine Leflaive Chardonnay!" Lorelei shouts as she yanks the bottle away from Paige's lips.

"Lorelei, fire up the Batmobile. We're going on a field trip," I tell her as she glares at Paige.

"Yes!" Paige shouts as she gets up from the couch and wraps her arms around me.

"What? No. Absolutely not. We are not going anywhere."

Paige and I look at each other and all of the wine I've consumed makes it perfectly acceptable that she's hugging me and in my personal space.

"Where are we going? Will there be penises?" she whispers with her chin on my shoulder.

"No, no penises. Better."

"Better than penises? I don't understand," Paige replies.

"We're going to my dad's office to fuck up Griffin's world," I inform her with an evil smile on my face.

"Okay, not that I'm condoning this nonsense, but how is going to your dad's office going to affect Griffin in any way?" Lorelei asks as she sets the bottle of wine down.

"Because, my dear, Griffin has a desk at my dad's office now. A desk and a computer. And files. And notes. Notes on whatever case he's currently working on."

"I still don't get it. Will we see his penis there?" Paige questions.

I ignore Paige and stare directly at Lorelei. Lorelei hates men. Lorelei hates it that Griffin might be using me to get what he wants. I shush the nagging voice in the back of my head telling me that Griffin wants *me*. Lorelei will understand my need to do whatever I can to get the jump on him and win this bet. He can't have me. I cannot be had!

She lets out a huge sigh and stares up at the ceiling for a few minutes before shaking her head at me.

"Fine. But you two are sitting in the backseat and not saying a word the entire trip there. And if we get caught, I don't know you."

Twenty minutes later I'm unlocking the door to my dad's office and creeping inside in the dark with Paige clutching the back of my shirt.

"Don't make a sound," I whisper to her as I move slowly into the room and try to feel my way around. My shin connects with a chair and I let out a yelp.

"SHHHHHHHHH!" Paige warns.

The pitch-black room is suddenly swathed in bright, fluorescent lighting as Lorelei flips the switch by the door.

"Is there a reason why you two are lurking around in the dark like burglars? You have a key, Kennedy. It's not breaking and entering if you have a key." She walks past the two of us crouched low to the ground.

"You are totally killing my buzz," I inform her as I stand up fully and move away from Paige to the spare desks in the back of the room that my dad reserves for his part-time bounty hunters.

Glancing between the three of them, I spot Griffin's black leather jacket draped over the chair of the desk closest to the wall.

"This is it. This is his desk," I tell the girls as I pull out the chair and have a seat.

"Ooooh, is this his jacket? It smells delicious. He wears yummy cologne," Paige sighs as she leans over and takes a big whiff of the coat.

"Focus, Paige."

She moves around me and perches on the edge of the desk.

"What exactly are we looking for? A to-do list with your name at the top of it? Kiss Kennedy—check. Give her an orgasm in her father's bathroom—check, check," Paige says as she riffles through the papers on top of the desk.

"Just see if you can find any leads on McFadden. Something we don't have . . . I'm guessing he has the same contacts I do, but you never know." I begin opening drawers and going through files while Lorelei flips through some phone messages next to the computer.

After fifteen minutes of searching, we don't find squat. Leaning back in the chair, I kick the edge of the desk with my boot and curse loudly.

"There's nothing here. This was a total bust," I complain.

I don't know what I expected to find here. Like Griffin would really leave something out that would lead us right to McFadden. If he had that information, he would be using it himself. And if this whole seduction thing he has going on with me is all a trick, I'm pretty sure he wouldn't leave any evidence behind to confirm that fact. Once again, I'm back to being irritated with all men.

"It's not a total bust," Paige tells me with a wag of her perfectly waxed eyebrows as she holds up a letter opener and a bottle of superglue.

"Whatever you're thinking of doing, don't," Lorelei warns her as she tries to take the items out of Paige's hands.

Paige moves out of her reach and around to the front of the desk. "So we didn't find anything we can use against Griffin, no big deal. We can still fuck things up for him."

She gives me a sinister, calculating grin and suddenly, I remember why we're friends.

"Kennedy, do not stoop to that level. You're better than this," Lorelei pleads with me.

It's a really nice statement for her to make, but I am not better than this. I'm struggling with the fact that Griffin may have diddled me so I lose the bet. And I'm losing my mind because during each of the times I've been wrapped around him, all I've been able to think about is how *right* it felt and how I couldn't imagine being anywhere else ever again.

Plus, I've had about eleventy-four glasses of wine tonight and my decision-making skills aren't exactly up to par.

Reaching my hand out toward Paige, I join the dark side. "I'll take the letter opener, you take the glue."

GD wine-addled brain.

CHAPTER 15

His palm slides up my bare thigh, pulls my leg back, and hitches it over his hip. I can feel every solid inch of his naked body against my back and I burrow closer to him until his erection is nestled against my ass.

"I've wanted you like this for eighteen years," he murmurs against the side of my neck before nibbling on my skin with his teeth.

I want to tell him not to say things like that, because it's totally going to kill the mood, but I can't find my voice when the tip of his penis slides against my opening.

"You know that's a total lie, right? I'm just saying things like this to you so I can catch McFadden," he whispers as he slowly starts to push himself inside me.

I want to pull away and smack the grin right off his face that I know is there, but he feels too good between my legs and my body has suddenly lost its ability to move.

He teases me by pushing just a little bit inside me and then pulling right back out and I groan loudly in protest.

"Shhhh, it's okay. I'll make you feel good, gorgeous. I'll make you come until you can't remember your name and then leave you here in bed to go get McFadden. Because you know I've known the entire time exactly where he is. I just wanted to see you race around trying to beat me. You'll never win. You should just accept that."

Alarms are going off in my head and I really should try harder to get out of this fucking bed, but he has a magical penis and I'm pretty sure he's using voodoo on me. I can't move and I can't speak. I should be concerned with this. I should be screaming obscenities at him, but when I open my mouth, nothing comes out but another groan.

He starts to push in deeper and it feels so good that I don't care about anything but finally having him inside me. What is wrong with me? More alarms are going off and they sound like bells ringing. Where are the bells coming from? They get louder and louder as he continues to whisper taunts in my ear.

With all of the strength I can muster, I finally make my arm move and reach out to smack away whatever that ringing sound is. My hand clutches something small and as he pulls out of me and readies himself to slam his way back home, I find my voice and scream for all I'm worth.

"YOU SCUM-SUCKING RAT BASTARD ASSHOLE! I HOPE YOUR PENIS FALLS OFF!"

"Well, good morning to you too," Griffin says with a chuckle.

Blinking my eyes into focus, I bolt up in bed and frantically look around, realizing I'm all alone with my cell phone up to my ear.

A dream? It was a fucking dream?

"I'm pretty sure I'm the one who should be screaming curses at this point," he says through the phone line while I try to shake the dream from my head. "Any idea how all of the keys on my computer got switched around and glued in the wrong place?"

At least that part wasn't a dream.

"Or maybe you know how two-hundred Post-it notes with pictures of penises drawn on them were glued to every inch of my desk," he deadpans.

Oops.

In my dream, I *couldn't* speak. Now that I'm awake, I just don't want to. Yes, I know I behaved a little childishly last night, but it wasn't my fault. It was the wine's fault.

"Really, it's no big deal that since I don't look at my fingers when I type, I sent out an e-mail to the state police that said 'gfpwq7 exclamation point asterisk' and my e-mail signature said 'Griffin Crawford, King of All Penises,'" he adds.

"Well, it serves you right for not proofing your e-mails before you send them," I finally say.

I hear him sigh on the other end of the line and I almost feel a little bad about our drunken escapade last night.

"Kennedy?"

When he says my name so soft and sweet I forget all about the bad dream I had.

"Yeah?" I reply quietly with a small smile on my face.

"Sleep with one eye open, babe. Game on."

I hear the silence of the ended call in my ear and for the first time in my life, I'm dreading getting out of bed and going to work.

This is not going to end well.

———

I spent the next day and a half interviewing anyone and everyone McFadden ever knew, including all of his childhood friends. No one had seen or heard from him in months and they couldn't give me anything to go on as far as finding him. On top of that huge waste of time, I couldn't stop looking over my shoulder waiting for Griffin to jump out from behind a bush and taser me to get back at me for that little superglue stunt we pulled.

Walking into Fool Me Investigations with a jumbo-size hazelnut coffee in my hand, I'm immediately assaulted by the sounds of phones ringing off the hook and Paige running back and forth between desks to answer them.

"Yes, I have your name and number and someone will call you back shortly. Yes, I wrote down that this is an emergency. Okay. Yes, we have a blonde that works here—why does that matter?" Paige asks into the phone as her pen pauses on the phone message pad. "Eeeeew, that's disgusting! What is wrong with you?"

She slams the phone down and stalks over to me, clutching a stack of messages in her hand.

"What the hell is going on?" I ask her as the phone she just hung up immediately starts to ring again and when I glance at the phone console on my desk, I see that all twelve lines are lit up and blinking angrily.

"This has been going on since I walked through the door an hour ago. People are calling for our services left and right. And let me tell you something, the things they are asking for are illegal in fifteen states," she tells me.

Grabbing the messages out of her hand, I skim through them and see that each and every one is asking for an immediate request to fix our back door.

"What the hell? Is our door broke? Are these all locksmiths?" I ask her.

"I don't know. Whenever I ask them they just laugh and tell me they want the special that's in the ad. Did you run an ad?"

I did place an ad in the local newspaper that was going to start running this week, but it was for 10 percent off for first-time customers. This makes no sense.

"Sleep with one eye open, babe. Game on."

Griffin's parting words on the phone this morning run through my head.

"Oh no," I whisper as the door opens and I see my dad walk in with the morning paper in his hands.

"Kennedy, if you needed money, you could have come to me," he says.

I snatch the paper out of his hand and flip to the classifieds. Right smack in the middle of the page is FOOL ME ONCE in big, bold letters. Underneath are the words "Looking for a good time?! Call Fool Me Once at 555-205-7201 for all of your escort needs. We have blondes, brunettes, and redheads. Make sure to ask about the Busted Back Door Special!"

"SON OF A BITCH!" I shout as I crumble up the paper and throw it in the trash.

"The guys at the VFW all want to know if they can get a friends-and-family discount. Tell me the truth, Kennedy. Is this business a front for prostitution?" my dad demands. "Are you a *hooker*? And when did your back door get busted? Is that a euphemism for something?"

Before I can set him straight, I feel my phone vibrate in my back pocket. Pulling it out, I see Griffin's name on the display and I growl into the phone when I answer it. "You are in big, big trouble."

He laughs through the line and I clench my teeth so hard I'm afraid I might break a few off as I watch my dad waltz over to Lorelei's empty desk and answer one of the ringing lines.

"You want to pay how much? Wow. Let me get your name and number and get back to you," my dad tells the person on the other end of the line.

"Kennedy!" he whisper-yells to me as he covers the mouthpiece with his hand. "This guy says he'll pay fifteen hundred dollars to bust your back door. I don't know why he'd pay that much to break a door, but I'm going to tell him you're game. We can always get it fixed later. I didn't realize prostitutes made so much money for weird stuff. I thought they just gave happy endings. I'm in the wrong business. I should be a pimp."

I groan loudly at my dad as he goes back to his phone call.

"What's wrong, Kennedy? I thought you would appreciate the fact that business is booming," Griffin says.

"This is NOT funny, Griffin."

He laughs again and it takes everything in me not to throw my phone against the wall.

"No, you're right. It's not funny," he tells me in a moment of seriousness. "It's HILARIOUS! Sorry, I don't have time to talk. Just got a tip on McFadden and I'm pulling into the location he was spotted at. Talk to you soon. Go pick out something pretty to wear on our date. A dress would be perfect so I can stare at your gorgeous legs."

I hang up on him mid-laugh, walk over to my dad, snatch the phone away from his ear, and slam the receiver down.

"Heeeey, I was just in the middle of negotiating you a higher price for this back-door thing," he complains.

"Paige, get the state police on the line. Griffin e-mailed them this morning and now he's got a bead on McFadden. I need to find out where he is and get there ASAP," I tell her as I head for the door. "Dad, help Paige man the phones until Lorelei gets out of court. And for the love of all that is holy, stop making deals with these idiots."

"I hope when your back door gets busted and you make a bunch of cash you get in a better mood. You're too grumpy," my dad complains as I throw open the door and ignore Paige's hysterical laughter.

GD busting-back-door requests.

CHAPTER 16

It takes most of the day for Paige to finally get back to me on where Griffin is. Through her powers of persuasion, she found out that Griffin lied and he really wasn't about ready to nab McFadden when he called me earlier. He was just following a few leads and coming up empty, thank God. I really don't know how Paige did it, and I sort of don't want to know since it probably now involves free anal from one of us, but she was able to convince the police to send Griffin a text with the wrong address in it.

Since he was currently working with them on leads, it wouldn't be weird that they'd send him a text. When she called me with the news, all she told me was that when I got there, I should make sure to have my camera phone ready.

Pulling up to the Hyatt in Mishawaka, I call Paige as I make my way inside and step into the elevator.

"Are you sure this is the right place? Why did you send him to a hotel?" I ask her as I press the button for the third floor.

"One of my friends from college is having her bachelorette party there tonight. I may have called and told her that a man, matching Griffin's description, would be knocking on the door claiming to be a bounty hunter, but he's really a stripper," she informs me. "I also told her that no matter how much he denies it, she should just play along."

Oh no.

"Paige, you didn't."

The elevator dings and the doors open up to the third floor and I can already hear screams and catcalls coming from a room at the end of the hall.

"You can thank me later. Take lots of pictures!"

I end the call and shove the phone into my pocket as the screaming and cheering gets louder and louder the closer I get to room 325. Taking a deep breath, I knock loudly on the door. It's immediately flung open and a woman wearing a tiara and a sash that reads BRIDE TO BE greets me with a huge smile.

"Yaaaaay, another guest! You're just in time," she squeals as she grabs my arm and drags me into the room. All I see is a group of twenty or so drunk women huddled in a circle.

The bride-to-be shoves a few of the women aside and pulls me front and center of the circle and my mouth drops open when I see Griffin sitting in a hotel chair shirtless, with a pink feather boa draped around his neck, swatting away hands that are reaching for the button of his jeans.

"Seriously, ladies, it's flattering that you think I'm a stripper, but I really need to get back to work." He tries to get up from the chair and five women all huddle behind him, shoving him back down in his seat by pushing on his shoulders.

"Wow, you guys are freakishly strong," he mutters as one of the girls gets down on her knees by his feet and starts untying his boot to the tune of Kid Rock's "Cowboy."

I really need to help him. It's all fun and games until some other woman tries to undress him. Watching them manhandle him is making me stabby. I'm kind of struck dumb by the sight of him with his shirt off. He doesn't have a six-pack—he has a ninety-five-pack. And when did he get a tattoo above his left pec? It's the United States Army insignia and I have the sudden urge to run my fingers over it. And then my tongue.

"Um, excuse me," I say loudly to the group at large.

No one hears me except for Griffin. He looks over the head of some woman wearing a headband with a giant plastic penis on it who is currently motorboating his crotch and raises his eyebrows at me.

I'm not going to lie; I feel a little ashamed of my actions now that he's glaring at me. This whole payback idea was stellar after a few bottles of wine. Now that I'm sober and the entire town thinks I'm a call girl and the bachelorette party will most likely pass around Griffin's phone number to everyone they know to recommend his stripping services? Not so much.

"Ladies!" I try again, shouting as loud as I can. A few of them turn to look at me and are none too happy that I took their attention away from the main event.

Raising my hands in a please-don't-kill me way, I try to reason with them.

"Sorry to interrupt, but this guy really isn't a stripper. It was a big misunderstanding. If you'll just let me get him out of here, you guys can go back to your partying," I explain to them.

"Is this part of the show? I think we're supposed to just play along, isn't that what Paige told us?" one of the girls whispers to someone behind me.

"Ooooooh, she's probably a stripper too! I've never seen a female stripper!" someone shouts from the other side of the room.

I start shaking my head frantically back and forth when everyone's attention is suddenly on me, giving Griffin the opportunity to get up out of his chair untouched. He walks through the throng of women who are eyeing me up and down lecherously and I hold his arm, pulling him toward me for protection.

"I'm sorry. I swear to God, I had nothing to do with this. Help me get out of here with my clothes on and we'll call a truce," I whisper to him in a panic as a hand smacks my ass.

"TAKE IT OFF, GIRLFRIEND!" someone screams.

Griffin wraps one arm around my waist, pulls my body up against his naked torso, and stares down at me with a calculating grin.

"So now you want to call a truce. I don't think so, honey. I think you should do as the ladies say and take it off!" he yells.

Twenty sets of arms go up in the air as they all start chanting. "Take it off! Take it off! Take it off!"

Aside from the fact that this is the most mortifying event in the history of my life, I can't help but enjoy the feel of Griffin's arm around me. I want to snuggle into the heat of his half-naked body. Even if he IS trying to throw me to the wolves.

As I smack random female hands away from the buttons of my formfitting, button-down black shirt, Griffin takes notice of the panicked look on my face and finally decides to come to my aid instead of instigating the drunk masses.

"All right, ladies, show's over. We really do need to get going," he shouts as he starts to walk backward through the crowd, pulling me along with him.

"But we want to see naked people!" someone argues and the crowd starts to boo and glare at us.

Jesus, who knew drunken bachelorettes were so angry?

There's a knock at the door and Griffin turns away from me to open it as I hope and pray that it's hotel security. I have a feeling these bitches aren't going to let us out of here alive.

The door opens and my father stands there in the hotel hallway with one eyebrow raised questioningly.

"Paige sent me. She said you might need my help," he tells Griffin as he takes in the scene behind us. Let's just say, I'm pretty sure my father has never seen so many fake penis products in his entire life. The woman with the light-up penis earrings may just put him over the edge.

"A SILVER FOX!" the bride-to-be shouts when she sees my father.

I cover my ears and cringe as the screams of approval make it to new heights.

A group of screaming and giggling women shove Griffin and me out of the way, grab on to my dad's arm and drag him into the room. I don't feel the need to save my father because he's a hard-ass. There's no way he'll let this go on for much longer; he won't have the patience for it.

The women are fawning all over him at this point, running their hands through his hair and kissing his cheeks. Any second now he's going to yell at all of them to back the fuck up.

Any second now . . .

"No, there must be some confusion. That's my daughter and she's not a stripper," my dad tells them with a stern look as they start asking him questions about his "stripper partners."

I sigh in relief that this will all be over soon and we can get the hell out of here.

"No, I'm serious. She's not a stripper. She's a hooker."

"Oh dear God," I mutter as they push my dad into the chair Griffin recently vacated and one woman straddles his lap.

I can't look. This is just . . . Oh my God . . . I'm going to puke.

"Griffin! Do something!" I scold him as I point angrily in my dad's direction while he looks up happily at the woman giving him a lap dance.

"Hey, Buddy! You need some help over there?" Griffin yells across the room to my dad.

"Nope. I got it under control. You two run along now. Go do some talking or something. Or better yet, go bust Kennedy's back door and pay her for it so she gets in a better mood," he yells back.

Griffin salutes my dad with a chuckle, grabs my hand, and pulls me out of the room. The door closes behind us just as a cheer erupts from inside and I can only imagine what is currently being done to my father.

GD drunk bachelorettes.

CHAPTER 17

A ll I know is, he didn't come home until three in the morning and he fell asleep with a huge-ass grin on his face. And I'm pretty sure I saw stripper glitter sparkling in his hair when the light hit it. What the hell happened?" my brother Bobby asks Ted as he loads a round of bullets into his service pistol and takes aim at the paper target ten yards away.

I walk up behind them at the tail end of their conversation and try not to think about what could have put such a big smile on my dad's face the previous night after Griffin and I left the hotel.

Every week since Bobby moved back in with my dad, the three of us meet at the indoor shooting range and throw out career ideas to him. It looks like this week Bobby's future is not going to be the main topic of discussion.

I clear my throat softly behind them so as not to startle them— never a good idea with people holding loaded weapons. Ted turns around, puts his gun on the ledge, and immediately wraps his arm around my neck and tugs me into a headlock, rubbing his knuckles against my scalp.

"What up, sis? Ready to get your ass kicked today?" Ted says with a laugh as I punch my fists into his side until he finally lets me go.

"Jesus, Ted, grow up," I complain as I stand back up and rub my sore head. We both stand silently in the lane at the indoor shooting range and watch Bobby fire off a few rounds, all but two hitting the center target.

"So, what's new with you? Aside from the fact that you're now a prostitute and Dad has decided to open a strip club?" Bobby asks as he steps back out of the lane and gestures for Ted to go next.

"Funny," I tell him with a smack to his upper arm. "I'm still trying to catch this fucking bail jumper while attempting NOT to strangle Griffin in the process."

Ted takes aim and unloads his clip into the target. Buddy laughs when half of them go wild and pierce the outer circle of the target.

"Son of a bitch! Something must be wrong with this gun. Here, you do something with it." Ted steps back and I reach my hand out for it.

"Go easy on Griffin. He's good people," Ted tells me and I load the clip with more rounds.

With a roll of my eyes, I lift my arms up, take a deep breath, and begin firing when I exhale. All but one bullet hits the center target.

"Ooooh, I do believe that makes me the winner," I gloat.

"I don't understand how you always beat us when WE taught you how to shoot," Buddy grumbles.

"Oh, I almost forgot. I got some information about your guy, McFadden," Ted tells me as he pulls a folded-up piece of paper out of his back pocket.

Taking it from his hand and putting the gun down on the ledge, I scan the information.

"Back when he was a teenager, he got popped for marijuana possession. The file was sealed because he was a minor at the time, but luckily, I know people," he informs me as Bobby steps up behind me and reads over my shoulder.

"He took the rap for some guy named Steven Lawson. They grew up together in the same neighborhood and were best friends," Bobby reads aloud.

"We already got this information and looked into the name Steven Lawson to question him and there weren't any hits on him. I questioned the friends of his I could find, but Steven Lawson didn't have a current address listed and none of the old friends remembered that name. What does this have to do with anything now?" I ask Ted as I look up from the paper.

"You're lucky I went on a date with one of the file clerks at the courthouse and completely blew her mind last week," Ted tells us with an arrogant grin.

"Shut up and get to the point," I warn him.

"Fine. Buzzkill. Steven Lawson changed his name after he got out of juvie. He now goes by the name Sven Mendleson."

My mouth drops open and my arm automatically reaches out and punches Ted in the arm. "Shut the fuck up. Are you serious?"

"Owww," Ted complains as he rubs the spot on his arm. "Serious as a heart attack, dude."

"I'm confused. Who the hell is Sven Mendleson?" Bobby asks as he takes the paper out of my hands and reads through it again.

"I asked Ward about Sven. He's some annoying guy who does shit to Kennedy's hair and wouldn't shut up about the fact that when McFadden showed up at his salon, he put his life on the line trying to apprehend him," Ted explains with a roll of his eyes. "Ward's pissed now that he knows Steven and Sven are the same person."

"That rat bastard. He let McFadden get away on purpose. I'm going to kick his ass."

"Slow down there, rough rider. If Sven Mendleson is Steven Lawson, you need to tread lightly. This guy isn't someone you mess with. He's kind of a big deal in the pot world," Ted warns.

"Seriously? You have got to be kidding me. There is no way that little asshole with the fake accent is a big deal in anything. He's probably been hiding McFadden all this time. Son of a bitch, I'm going to kill him!"

I start pacing back and forth in the small booth with thoughts of homicide by hair dye swirling through my brain.

"I'm telling you, Kennedy, do NOT go into this alone. Now that the police are aware of the connection between Sven and Steven, they are taking control. You agree to let the police handle this or I go to Griffin and make him hold you hostage until it's settled. I only gave you this information so that you'd stop with all the wild-goose chases," Ted warns me.

"Kennedy might actually like being held hostage by Griffin," Bobby says with a laugh, which earns him his very own punch in the arm.

"So what's the deal with Griffin? Are you guys dating or what?" Ted presses the button to bring the paper target forward. "And more importantly, are you going to be charging him by the hour or by the orgasm?"

They both start laughing like idiots and I cross my arms in front of me and glare at them.

"No! We are not dating, nor will we EVER be dating."

Ted unhooks the target from the clips and sets it aside before attaching a new, clean one and hitting the button to send it back.

"What's your problem with him? He's a good guy and he roots for Notre Dame. What more could you ask for?" Buddy demands.

"He kind of told me he's had a thing for me for eighteen years. Which I know is a total lie and he just did that to throw me off so he could get to McFadden first," I complain.

Both of the boys are silent for so long after I say this that an uneasy feeling creeps over me. They are never this quiet. Ever.

"What?" I ask, looking back and forth between them.

"Nothing, it's nothing," Ted says as he picks up the pistol and busies himself loading it.

I walk up and snatch the gun out of his hand and smack it back down on the ledge.

"Speak."

"Ruff!" Bobby pipes up from behind me.

Without taking my eyes off Ted, I reach back and smack Bobby in the stomach, feeling satisfied when he lets out a painful *oof.*

Ted has always been the easiest one to break. Even when we were little and he was eight and I was four. All I had to do was glare at him and he would sing like a canary. Narrowing my eyes and putting my hands on my hips, it only takes a few seconds before Ted bursts.

"I don't understand how in all these years you never noticed that he TOTALLY has a thing for you. He's been in love with you since high school and only joined the army because you did and he wanted to make sure you were safe and then made sure to live close enough to you to keep an eye on you. Haven't you ever wondered why he never got married himself? YOU'RE his dream girl, not stupid Megan Fox. Alex is such an asshole that he might have just married you so Griffin couldn't have you."

Ted finally shuts up and lets out a huge sigh of relief at having unloaded a huge pile of shit right at my feet that I have no idea what to do with. This cannot really be happening right now.

"Jesus, Ted. When did you grow ovaries?" Bobby complains with a sad shake of his head.

"Whew, that felt good. That's been like a brick on my chest for *years,*" Ted says.

A smile. Like it's no big deal. I don't even know which part of that confession to process first. Could it be possible that Alex only married me so Griffin couldn't? Thinking back over our marriage and all of the ups and downs, mostly downs, it could very well be true. And if Griffin really was in love with me, why the hell didn't he ever say anything sooner? I mean seriously? Aside from my daughters, whom I wouldn't trade for the world, there is nothing else even remotely memorable about my marriage to Alex.

"This is BULLSHIT!" I finally yell with a stomp of my foot. "He had plenty of time to make his move. Prom. FUCKING PROM! I had a crush on him. I was thinking about dumping Alex for him. We were going to go to prom together and everything would have been beautiful, but he ditched me and I married Alex!"

Bobby cocks his head at me. "Wasn't that like, twenty years ago? Who cares about prom? Let it go."

"Let it go?! LET IT GO?! I CARE ABOUT PROM! There is no statute of limitations on being angry about getting ditched two days before prom," I argue indignantly.

Don't judge me. I don't care if it was *eighty* years ago. I had bought a dress and matching shoes. A DRESS. I was going to wear a fucking dress for him and most likely give him my virginity. I'm allowed to be angry about that for as long as I want. Plus, being angry about prom helps me to not think about the fact that he's been carrying a torch around for me all of these years and never said anything.

Why the hell would anyone have a thing for me that long? I'm nothing special. I'm just me. Griffin is gorgeous, funny, sweet, helpful, a good listener, a great friend, beats up my ex-husband for me, and loves my girls unconditionally. He even puts up with my insane family. I love that about him. I love everything about him, even his stupid, cocky attitude.

Son of a bitch!

All thoughts of Steven Lawson/Sven Mendleson fly from my mind. When in the hell did I fall in love with Griffin Crawford??

GD Griffin Crawford!

CHAPTER 18

⌒

Sitting all alone in the dark on the floor of Fool Me Once at midnight on a Wednesday should tell you just how fantastic I'm doing right now. As soon as I left the shooting range, I sent a text to Alex and told him he was keeping the girls for a few more days because I had work to do.

It wasn't completely a lie. I did have work to do. But I also had thoughts to think. Lots of thoughts. Important thoughts. Thoughts that couldn't be thunk with a twelve-year-old complaining that I'm the worst mom in the world and a nine-year-old begging me to send her to military school.

It's not their fault their father is an asshole. They deserve a man in their lives who will put them first. Griffin would put them first. Griffin *does* put them first. He also manages to somehow put me first as well. How could I have been so blind?

As I continue to beat myself up, my thoughts are interrupted by a soft knock on the glass door to the building. Pushing myself up off the floor, I rest my hand on the butt of the gun in my holster as I head toward the door and wonder who the hell would be knocking this late at night. I stop in my tracks when I look up and see Griffin standing on the other side of the glass.

How the hell did he even know I was here?

The streetlight on the sidewalk shines down on him and I cover the remaining distance to the door in a trance, my eyes never leaving his. He stares down at me as I reach up and turn the deadbolt on the door and push it open for him. I take a few steps back to give him room to come in and he relocks the door without looking away from me.

Why did I never see this before? Why did I never notice the way he looks at me: like I'm the most important person in his world? Why did I never appreciate him and love him like he deserved?

"I drove by your house but didn't see your car. Took a chance that you'd be here."

He opens his mouth to say something else and I quickly reach my hand up and place it over his lips. His eyes soften as he looks down at me.

"No more talking. Not right now," I whisper to him.

Right now I don't want to argue with him and I don't want to hash out all of the details. I just want to feel.

Griffin nods his head in agreement and I drop my hand.

Come tomorrow, I am most likely going to do something really, really stupid. Something I swore to Ted that I would let the police handle. Tonight, I want to do something smart.

Standing up on my tiptoes, I wrap my arms around his neck and pull his head down to mine. When our lips connect, I can't help but sigh in relief. It feels like forever since I kissed him last and I don't even care that I'm thinking like a sappy, lovesick girl right now. I *am* a sappy, lovesick girl.

Griffin's hands grab onto my hips and he effortlessly lifts me up against him. I wrap my legs tightly around his waist as he begins walking us through the office.

I move away from his mouth to pull my shirt up and off my body, flinging it into the middle of the room before fusing my lips to his, our tongues tangling immediately. My back is suddenly slammed against a wall and I don't even care when I hear a painting fall off and crash to the floor. Griffin leaves me leaning against the wall and sinks down onto his knees in front of me, pushing my jeans, along with my underwear, down to my ankles in one rough yank.

I have just enough time to pull my feet out of my jeans and clutch his hair before his mouth is on me. There's nothing slow and gentle about the way he delves between my legs and that's perfectly fine with me. He devours me with his lips, tongue, and fingers all at once, everywhere. With each swipe of his tongue and swirl of his fingers I'm pushed closer and closer into a mindless ball of need. My hips thrust frantically against him as I hold his head in place, aching to reach my release that throbs so close.

With his lips firmly attached to my clit and a thrust of two of his fingers inside me, I explode fast and hard around him, letting my head thump back against the wall while I shout his name. As my orgasm ebbs and flows out of me, his tongue leisurely slides against me until I'm spent. I let go of the death grip I have on his hair and he kisses his way up my body until he's standing before me.

I love this man. And not just because he gave me yet another mind-blowing orgasm. I love him because he's Griffin.

Grabbing on to the hem of his shirt, I yank it up and over his head, dropping it by our feet before quickly unsnapping his jeans. Reaching my hand inside his pants, I palm his thick erection.

"Fuck, Kennedy," he groans as he leans his body into mine and buries his head against my neck. I slide my hand up and down his smooth length, firm and slow. "We need to stop. I am not taking you up against a wall. A bed. We need a bed."

His voice is broken and filled with need and it's the hottest sound I've ever heard. Squeezing him tighter and moving my hand faster, I distract him long enough to reach down with my other hand and push his jeans far enough down his hips so that his cock is no longer constricted.

"Fuck the bed. We can do that later," I tell him as I hitch one leg around his hip and use my thigh muscles to pull him in closer.

I move my hand out of the way as his erection slides against me. One of his arms wraps around my waist and holds me tightly and the other hand smacks against the wall by my head to brace himself. We both let out a groan and he drops his forehead against mine, holding it there while he pushes and pulls his length through my wetness.

"I know you said no talking, and that's fine. You don't have to talk. In fact, I don't want you to say anything," he tells me as he slides the head of his cock back and forth over my sensitive clit. "But you need to know, right here, right now, that I love you, Kennedy O'Brien. I have *always* loved you."

It's a good thing he told me not to speak because I couldn't say anything right now if I wanted to. I can feel my eyes welling up with tears and I try to blink them away as I stare up at him. Without saying a word, I move my hands up to either side of his face and pull him against my mouth. I tell him everything I can't say out loud with my lips and tongue. I pour everything into this kiss and I hope to God he knows and can feel it. I moan into his mouth when he pulls his hips back slightly and then slowly pushes himself inside me. The dream I had about this moment the other night pales in comparison to the real thing.

He's thick and full inside me, his body is pressed up against me, and his hands move slowly over every inch of me that he can reach. I feel him everywhere and when he begins plunging in and out of me, I match his movements thrust for thrust until he's pounding into me at a feverish pace. We're slamming against the wall so hard that I'm waiting to feel myself crash through the drywall at any minute. I don't care if we tear this wall down or the entire building comes crashing down around us.

Another orgasm barrels through me at a shocking speed, this one just as explosive as the first one. I try to move my mouth away from Griffin's so I can scream and moan my satisfaction, but he keeps his lips pressed to mine and swallows my cries. His tongue pushes slow and deep into my mouth as each wave of my release washes through me. Within seconds he slams into me one last time and holds himself still as he quickly follows me with his own orgasm. It's my turn to hold his lips against mine as he moans into my mouth and pulses inside of me. He rocks his hips against me slowly until his body sags against mine and he pulls his mouth away so we can both breathe heavily.

I rest my cheek on his shoulder and hold him as tightly to me as possible while I catch my breath and he presses several kisses to the top of my head.

After a few minutes, he pulls out of me, scoops me up into his arm, and carries me into the back room, where there's a very roomy couch that is in desperate need of being broken in.

No more words are exchanged between us for the rest of the night. We might not have a bed like Griffin wanted, but that couch definitely served us well.

It served us well four more times before we both passed out.

GD man and his stamina.

CHAPTER 19

I'm a coward.

Go ahead and say it. I already know it's true, so you may as well validate me. I got dressed and left the office at the crack of dawn. I snuck out of there with Griffin still naked and asleep on the couch.

I know I shouldn't have done it. I know I should have woken him up and told him I love him. Hell, I should have told him last night before we had sex the third or fourth time. I'm stubborn and pigheaded and fiercely independent. Griffin already knows this about me so when he wakes up and finds me gone, he shouldn't be too surprised.

All of this dating nonsense revolved around a bet. A stupidly sweet bet that Griffin came up with as a way to get back into my life, but still. A bet's a bet and I do not lose bets. Plus, if I'm going to date anyone, it's going to be because I choose to do it and not because I had to do it to hold up my end of the bargain.

In the wee hours of the morning, when I can still feel the scratch of Griffin's five o'clock shadow between my thighs and every muscle in my body aches deliciously from overuse, I am pulling into the driveway of a farmhouse in the middle of bum-fuck nowhere.

According to the printout Ted gave me yesterday, this sprawling ten-acre farm surrounded by cornfields on all sides is owned by our very own man of the hour: Sven Mendleson. AKA Steve Lawson. AKA lying sack of shit, bail-jumper-hiding, drug-dealing thorn in my side.

Pulling up right in front of the huge wraparound porch, I put my Explorer in park, turn off the engine, and step out onto the gravel drive. I don't see any other cars anywhere and while this should put me a little bit at ease that the place isn't crawling with twitchy potheads and dealers picking up their stash, it leaves me feeling just a tiny bit uneasy. As I slowly make my way up the steps, I double-check my gun to make sure it's fully loaded before sliding it into my holster. Taking a deep breath, I reach up and knock on the door, keeping one hand resting on the butt of my gun just in case.

I don't hear any noise on the other side of the door, and I take a moment while I wait to look around the yard and keep an eye out for any movement. Not seeing anything of concern, I reach back up to knock again when the door is opened before my knuckles can make contact with the wood.

"'Sup," the twentysomething guy in front of me says with a jerk of his chin.

As I take in his blue Cookie Monster T-shirt, ratty jeans, fuzzy yellow duck slippers, and open bag of Cheetos, I quickly decide this guy is most likely not going to be a threat to me. And going by his bloodshot eyes that he can barely keep focused on me, I'm going to guess the only threat he could possibly pose would be secondhand smoke.

"Hi, my name's Kennedy and I'm looking for Martin McFadden. Have you seen him?"

He stares at me while he reaches one hand into his bag of Cheetos and brings one up to his mouth, crunching slowly.

"Weird old dude who believes in aliens, about this tall?" he asks, holding his hand up to his chin.

"Yep, that's him," I reply with an excited nod of my head.

"Nope, never heard of him," he tells me, shoveling a handful of Cheetos in his mouth.

Oh, for the love of God.

"Look, I don't really care what's going on here—I just want McFadden. Tell me where he is, I will take him with me quietly, and you can go back to eating your way through the junk-food aisle of the grocery store," I plead with him.

"Steve will be really pissed if I talk. I wish I had some Peanut Butter Cap'n Crunch right now." He stares dejectedly into his bag of Cheetos.

"I promise, Steve won't be pissed. And I will buy you *twenty* boxes of Peanut Butter Cap'n Crunch if you take me to McFadden."

I find it hard to believe the Steve/Sven I know could seriously get pissed about anything unless it has to do with bad hair, but I'm not about to tell this guy that.

"Peanut butter is delicious. Captain is crunchy. *Crunchy* is a funny word. I think Martin is in the snack making a kitchen," he tells me with a nod toward the back of the house.

Good lord, this guy needs to be the poster boy for why kids should stay off drugs.

Taking a step past him and into the living room while he stands there licking the Day-Glo orange cheese off his fingers, I hear the unmistakable sound of a gun being cocked and I stop in my tracks.

"Take your gun out of its holster and toss it onto the couch, slowly."

It's Sven, without the accent. I slowly turn around with my hands in the air and see him standing at the opening of the hallway with a .44 Magnum aimed right at my head. Holding that gun at me, he no longer looks like a hairdresser with a poodle named Mrs. Justin Bieber. Right now he looks like he would shoot me between the eyes without even blinking.

With one hand still up in the air, I slowly reach down with my other hand and gradually pull my gun out of its holster and do as he says, tossing it onto the couch cushions.

"Now, toss me your car keys," he demands.

Have I mentioned yet how stupid an idea this was coming here alone?

Sliding my hand into my front pocket, I pull my keys out and chuck them at him. He easily catches them with the hand not holding the gun and puts them in his own pocket.

"Hey, Stevie, are we all out of mayo? I looked in the pantry and I don't—"

McFadden walks into the room with Tinkerdoodle under his arm and stops speaking as soon as he sees the scene in front of him.

"What's going on? Oh my gosh, don't shoot her!" McFadden wails as he looks back and forth between me and the gun pointed at my face.

"Look Sven, Steve, whatever your name is, I don't want any trouble. I could care less what's going on here. I have a cousin who smokes pot for his glaucoma. Great stuff, excellent results. I just want to take McFadden in nice and peacefully so the bondsman can get his money back," I say.

"It's okay. Stevie won't hurt you, will you, Stevie? I'm finished with my life of crime. I've learned my lesson. The life of a thug is no life for me," McFadden says wearily as he starts to walk toward me.

Before he can even make it a few steps in my direction, Steve quickly reaches out and grabs hold of McFadden's arm, yanking him back so hard that he drops Tinkerdoodle to the floor. Steve keeps McFadden close to him and brings the gun up, pressing it right against McFadden's temple.

"STEVIE! What are you doing?! Oh my God, oh my God, oh my God," McFadden cries hysterically.

"I'm gonna go take a nap," the pothead over by the door suddenly announces before shuffling off down the hall in his duck slippers.

"I knew letting you hide out here would be a bad idea. Now the fucking cops are going to be swarming this place. Do you have any idea how much product I'm going to lose when they storm in here? How many millions of dollars are going to go right down the drain because you're a fuckup?" Steve yells angrily.

"Stevie, don't say things like that! I thought we were friends!" McFadden cries.

"Oh, shut up. We were never friends; I just tolerated you so you'd take the fall for me back in high school. And now look where that got me. A fucking cop here in my living room and thousands of pounds of weed in my basement," he growls, gesturing toward me with his gun.

I need to get McFadden away from this lunatic and get out of this house. How the hell am I going to do that without a gun?

Tinkerdoodle lets out a small little yip when her stares at McFadden go ignored and a thought pops into my head. It's not the brightest idea in the world, but I'm obviously not very full of bright ideas today, now, am I?

I'm hoping McFadden is pissed off enough at finding out our boy Steve here was never really his friend and he'll play along. Otherwise, we're all screwed.

"Hey, McFadden. Remember that day we hung out at the tailgating party and you made me a hamburger?" I ask him, staring pointedly down at Tinkerdoodle.

Come on, get the hint. Get the hint.

"Remember how *sweet* and *loving* Tinkerdoodle was with me before you left?"

I'm starting to lose my faith in this guy and Steve is beginning to look suspicious when I see the lightbulb go on in McFadden's brain.

I give him the tiniest of nods. He swallows thickly, squeezes his eyes closed, and screams, "TINKERDOODLE! ATTACK!"

Just like on tailgating day, Tinkerdoodle jumps to action in a blur of fur, snapping teeth, yapping barks, and flying spit as she charges at Steve's leg and clamps down on his ankle.

"SON OF A BITCH!" Steve screams in pain as he shoves McFadden away and tries to get the dog off his leg.

The pitter-patter of dog toenails echoes around us as Mrs. Justin Bieber flies into the living room to get in on the action. Luckily, she's decided to be a joiner, chomping her teeth down on Steve's other leg.

Without hesitation, I lunge forward, grab McFadden's arm, and drag him behind me as fast as I can toward the front door while both dogs bite down harder on Steve's leg and he shouts and flails around the living room trying to dislodge them.

We stumble out the front door and down the steps when it hits me that I don't have my keys and have no way to escape. I don't have time to worry about that right now though, because it won't be long before Steve comes racing out here after us, guns a-blazing.

Yanking McFadden in front of me, I shove him as hard as I can and scream at him to run.

"GO! Into the corn! Don't stop until I tell you!"

We sprint full speed the ten yards or so across the grass until we burst into the first row of corn, smacking stalks out of our way as we go and hearing the first sounds of a gun being fired in our direction.

I'm too busy running and looking over my shoulder to notice McFadden stop suddenly and I slam into the back of him, both of us stumbling forward.

"What the hell? Why are you stopping? KEEP GOING!" I yell at him as another shot echoes behind us, this one closer than the last.

"A crop circle," he whispers in wonder. "Oh my God, they've been here. They'll save us!"

Looking around him in irritation, I see a huge, matted-down area of cornstalks directly in front of us.

"For God's sake, get your shit together, man! We need to get the hell out of here!"

The hard, cold steel of the nose of a gun presses roughly into the back of my head and I realize we've just lost our chance at escaping.

GD crop circle.

CHAPTER 20

"Will you stop crying? Goddammit, you're giving me a head-ache," Steve complains to McFadden.

I have an unnatural urge to reach out and smack Steve upside the head. However, this wouldn't be a wise idea since he currently still has a gun aimed at me.

"Just tell me Tinkerdoodle is still alive!" McFadden sobs as he stands next to me in the middle of the "crop circle" where Steve forced us to walk.

Oh, don't worry about me with a GUN TO MY HEAD. The dog that you stole is perfectly fine, thank you very much.

"Hey, dude. I heard some shots. You need my help or something?"

Pothead waltzes into our little party with a gun in his hand, using the tip of it to scratch his head.

This just keeps getting better and better.

"It's about fucking time you got here. Keep an eye on Martin; this one's all mine," Steve says as he wraps his fingers tightly around my upper arm and digs the gun back into the side of my head.

"You couldn't just forget about Martin and go on your merry way. You had to keep digging, didn't you? Now you're both going to die," Steve threatens.

McFadden begins wailing embarrassingly loud and Steve and I both groan in annoyance. At least we're in agreement on something:

McFadden is irritating. But not so much that he needs to be shot in the middle of a cornfield.

"Look, how about you just let him go and deal with me?" I ask him, trying to plead with the tiniest bit of humanity I hope he still has left in him.

"Sorry, no can do. I don't trust either of you. You're each getting a bullet to the brain."

Okay, maybe not. On to Plan B.

Except I don't have a Plan B. I'm pretty sure I didn't even have a Plan A.

"I don't think that will be necessary, Steve."

Pure elation and downright dread fight in the pit of my stomach when I hear the sound of Griffin's voice and the click of a gun that I'm pretty sure he has aimed at Steve's head right at this moment.

I'm so happy he's here that I want jump up and down and point and laugh in Steve's face. But I'm also scared to death that he's here right now. What if he gets hurt? Griffin can't get hurt just because of me. Especially when he doesn't even know I love him.

"What are you going to do, hotshot? Shoot both of us? In case you haven't noticed, there are two of us with guns and only one of you," Steve taunts Griffin.

We all turn at the same time and look at the pothead standing on the other side of me, swaying back and forth, twirling his gun through the air like he's writing his name with a Fourth of July sparkler.

"Oh, for fuck's sake, Gunnar, FOCUS!" Steve yells at him.

Gunnar? Note to self: Never name any future children that I may or may not have Gunnar. They will indeed be brainless twits.

Gunnar jumps into action, sort of, and stands at attention with his gun held up to his forehead and his chest puffed out.

As soon as I look away from him, I feel Steve remove the gun from the back of my head and in a flash, he twists around and pistol-whips Griffin against the side of his face, taking him by surprise. I watch as Griffin's gun goes flying through the air and he stumbles backward a few steps. He gains his footing and shakes the cobwebs from his head. With a growl, he ducks his head and charges right at Steve, tackling him to the ground like a linebacker.

McFadden stands in the middle of the clearing flapping his arms wildly and screaming as he jumps up and down in place like a six-year-old girl throwing a fit in the toy store.

While Gunnar is distracted by Steve and Griffin's scuffle and McFadden losing his ever-loving mind, I take that moment to pull my arm back and throw an uppercut. His eyes roll into the back of his head as soon as my fist makes contact and he crumbles to the ground at my feet.

I turn around with a satisfied look on my face when I see Steve kick both of his feet into Griffin's chest and send him soaring backward, knocking the wind out of him when he lands. While Griffin groans and tries to catch his breath, Steve rolls over and grabs one of the fallen guns, jumps up with blood dripping from his mouth and nose and aims the gun at me.

Pulling the slide back to load the first bullet into the chamber, he winks at me while I watch his finger tighten on the trigger. There's nothing I can do at this point but squeeze my eyes closed and brace myself for the pain.

I hear a loud yell of protest and fear that comes from Griffin, along with the unmistakable sound of the gun going off. What feels like a brick wall crashes into the side of me and I'm slammed down roughly into the dirt and broken cornstalks. I can't breathe with the heavy weight on top of me and all I can think about is that being shot hurts a whole fucking lot more than I thought it would.

Another shot goes off and it makes me flinch and finally open my eyes. When I don't see a white light or any golden gates, I realize I'm not dead. I'm flat on the ground with Griffin on top of me. "OH MY GOD, I SHOT HIM! Oh no, I'm going to puke. It's happening. Right now. I'm going to be sick," McFadden yells as he bends over at the waist and dry-heaves next to a screaming Steve who holds on to the bloody mess of what's left of the hand McFadden shot off.

"Are you okay? Are you hurt?" Griffin asks in a panic as he takes some of his weight off me and runs his hands over every inch of me, checking for bullet holes.

"Jesus, that just took ten years off my life," he whispers in my ear as he pulls me against him and I bury my face in his neck.

"Seriously, does no one even care that I'm throwing up over here? I need a cold washrag and some 7 Up," McFadden complains through his heaves.

As good as it feels to be wrapped in Griffin's arms, knowing that we're both safe and sound, there's something I need to do before this goes any further. With a sigh, I gently push Griffin off me and ignore the questioning look on his face as I get up and walk over to McFadden.

Patting him on the back with one hand as he gags, I reach into my back pocket with my other hand and pull out my zip ties. While he's busy retching, I pull his arms behind his back and secure them together with the pieces of plastic.

"I saved your life and this is the thanks I get?" McFadden complains as he stands up and struggles to move his arms.

I refrain from responding to him, on the grounds that it may result in me murdering him in cold blood in the middle of his precious crop circle. Instead, I leave him there to complain and walk back over to Griffin.

"So, I guess this means you won the bet. You don't have to go on a date with me now," he tells me with a cocky grin.

I smile sweetly right back at him. And then I punch him square in the jaw.

Satisfied that this stupid bet can stop looming over my head, I grab on to the front of his shirt, quickly haul him to me before he can complain and plant a kiss square on his mouth. After a few seconds, I pull away and give him my own cocky smile.

"How about we just call it a tie."

GD stalemate.

EPILOGUE

Two weeks later . . .

Putting on the finishing touches, I check myself in the mirror one last time and take a deep breath before exiting the bathroom. I walk out into the main area of Fool Me Once and stay silent for a few minutes as I watch my family and friends all standing around bickering with one another. Since I had a bunch of work to catch up on at the office, I brought my change of clothes with me so Griffin and I could leave for our date from here. Everyone said they were stopping by for a little congratulatory toast over McFadden's capture and that we all lived to tell the tale, but I'm pretty sure they had another reason for coming here tonight. I knew Griffin wouldn't be able to keep his mouth shut. I'm just thankful that Griffin still *has* a mouth to keep shut, no thanks to me and my idiocy out at the farm a few weeks ago. Thank God for my brother, Ted. As soon as Griffin woke up alone that morning and noticed me gone, he didn't hesitate to call my brother, who told him all about Sven/Steve and where he lived.

"I'm just saying, it could be a very lucrative side business," my dad states, taking a sip of champagne.

"I don't care how lucrative it is, Buddy. Prostitution is still illegal in Indiana," Lorelei tells him.

"Oh, speaking of whores, what's going on with that case of yours, Paige? Weren't you working on catching some slutty guy whose wife suspected him of cheating?" my brother Ted asks her while he pours some champagne in her glass.

In all the chaos, I totally forgot about our other two pending cases that Paige and Lorelei took while I was busy with McFadden. I watch in fascination as Paige's cheeks redden at my brother's question. She looks away from him and quickly downs the entire glass of champagne in one swallow.

"Guy? What guy? There's no guy. I don't know a guy. Who wants more champagne?" she asks, grabbing the bottle from Ted's hand and walks away from him.

Well, that was weird.

"Hey, Buddy, I have some work stuff I need you to sign," Uncle Wally says as he walks up to my dad and thrusts a paper and pen in his hands.

"What is this?" my dad demands as he scans the page.

"You don't need to read it, just sign it."

My dad huffs and continues reading.

"Of course I need to read it. I'm not signing something I haven't read."

"Oh, for God's sake, Buddy, just sign it!" Uncle Wally argues.

"This is the form to change the name of the business to Buddy Wally's Bail Bonds! You're a fucking lunatic!" my dad yells before throwing the pen at Uncle Wally's head.

"I'm going to punch you right in your arthritic hip, you old bastard!" Uncle Wally shouts back.

I swear to God, nothing ever changes around here. Rolling my eyes, I look away from my dad and uncle and see Griffin perched on the edge of my desk laughing at the scene unfolding in front of him.

It's been a long time since I've seen him in anything other than jeans and a T-shirt. His black dress pants and blue button-down shirt are a sight to behold. He's so gorgeous it takes my breath away.

And he's all mine.

After Tinkerdoodle was returned to her owners and McFadden was taken back to jail, I promised to give him regular updates on the state of Tinkerdoodle's well-being. It's the least I could do for him since he shot off a guy's hand for me.

Steve/Sven spent several days in the hospital to repair his mangled hand and is currently behind bars awaiting trial. Considering the amount of pot they found in his basement, minus the amount that Gunnar smoked all in one day, he's going to be in prison for a very long time. Paige has been considerably quiet about the fact that she has to find a new hairdresser now, which makes me wonder all over again what the hell is going on with her lately. That case with the cheating spouse should have been a piece of cake. I am absolutely going to talk to her about it. After tonight, of course.

With a deep breath, I step away from the wall and walk out into the room. The past few weeks have been a mess of activity, and Griffin and I haven't had any time alone. Since I got to punch him in the face that day on the farm, he told me it was only fair that I make good on my part of the bet. Hence the real reason why I believe everyone decided to congregate here tonight.

The arguing stops abruptly and everyone turns in my direction. I'm suddenly rethinking this whole idea as everyone in the room stares in fascination like I'm a zoo animal.

Griffin is the only one who moves as he pushes off my desk and walks over to me with a look of shock on his face.

"Jesus, have I mentioned lately how gorgeous you are?" Griffin asks as he takes in my short, red strapless dress and four-inch Jimmy Choo heels, courtesy of Paige. "You should wear dresses more often."

I smile at him and wrap my arms around his shoulders.

"If you wouldn't have ditched me two days before prom, you *could* have seen me in a dress long before this," I tell him.

"That was twenty years ago. Are you still holding a grudge about that?" he says with a laugh.

"Sorry, dude. I hate to inform you, but according to chicks, there is no statute of limitations on their anger over being ditched right before prom," Bobby tells him with a raise of his glass.

"Fine. I am deeply sorry for not taking you to prom. Seriously. You have no idea how sorry I am," he tells me softly.

I swallow hard and stare up at him, not even caring that I'm about to cry like a girl.

"It's okay. You're forgiven. And I'm deeply sorry for never noticing," I tell him in a rare moment of sweetness from myself. "I love you, Griffin."

He closes his eyes and lets out a sigh of relief before pressing his forehead against mine.

"Shame on you, Kennedy O'Brien, for making me wait so long to hear those words," he says with a chuckle before leaning down and kissing me while everyone in the room whistles and cheers around us.

ACKNOWLEDGMENTS

First and foremost, I'd like to thank my agent Jane Dystel for her unwavering support and belief in what I do.

To my editor Krista Stroever, thank you for making my first experience in traditional publishing an easy one, and for totally getting my humor!

To Donna and Chas, thank you for all of your hard work trying to organize my chaotic life. Without you, my email would be filled with spam and I'd never know what day it is.

James, Madelyn, and Drew, you love me even when I forget what day it is and don't shower or move from my spot on the front porch for days at a time. I love you more than anything else in this world, even if I call you by the wrong names.

A huge, heartfelt thank you to all of my fans will never suffice, but it's the best I can do right now. Your e-mails, Facebook posts, and all-around awesomeness amaze me every single day. You are the reason that all of this is possible, and I will be forever grateful that you took a chance on me.

There are entirely too many blogs out there that I owe my thanks to, but just know that I love and appreciate all of you for your constant support.

ABOUT THE AUTHOR

Tara Sivec is a *USA Today* best-selling author, wife, mother, chauffeur, maid, short-order cook, baby-sitter, and sarcasm expert. She lives in Ohio with her husband and two children and looks forward to the day when all three of them become adults and move out.

After working in the brokerage business for fourteen years, Tara decided to pick up a pen and write instead of shoving it in her eye out of boredom. She is the author of the Playing with Fire series and the Chocolate Lovers series. Her novel *Seduction and Snacks* won first place in the Indie Romance Convention Reader's Choice Awards 2013 for Best Indie First Book.

In her spare time, Tara loves to dream about all of the baking she'll do and naps she'll take when she ever gets spare time.

For more information on Tara Sivec's work, visit www.tarasivec.com